The phone rang in Sprig's office. He picked it up and spoke
scarcely a word, just listening, as someone talked to
him. At last Sprig said, quietly, and hung up.
He seemed pleased.

"That was Chicago. They've decided to bust Joe—they're beginning to

Rux asked: "What happened?"

"A two-bit Chi torpedo will be here on the midnight
plane."

Ochoa groaned. "How can they be that crude?"

Sprig only smiled, rubbing his bony hands together. "It
means we've got them on the ropes. And we're going to
keep them there."

"Don't they know," said Rux, "that a hood hasn't a
chance in Vegas?"

"If they did, they've forgotten," Sprig answered.
"Because they're playing right into my hands."

"Who's he supposed to kill—Joe?"

"Me," Sprig said. He was so happy, he got up and
paced the room. "Isn't that beautiful? They want revenge.
Sprig's bright red blood. Well, now it's juicy—good and
juicy."

"We meet him at the plane?" Ochoa asked.

"No. We'll just follow him. The man we want to nail isn't
the torpedo—it's the one who pays him and gives him his
instructions. Because he'll know who it is we're dealing
with—what group it is." He sighed. "Oh, I love this! Boys,
our work isn't without certain compensations now and then."

"A guy's coming to bump you off, and you love it," Rux
teased.

"Oh, I do, I do—nothing I like better than to see the
expression on their faces when you pull the rug out from
under them…"

No House LIMIT

by **Steve Fisher**

A HARD CASE CRIME NOVEL

A HARD CASE CRIME BOOK
(HCC-045)
July 2008

Published by

Dorchester Publishing Co., Inc.
200 Madison Avenue
New York, NY 10016

in collaboration with Winterfall LLC

ISBN 0-8439-5963-0
ISBN-13 978-0-8439-5963-5

Cover design by Cooley Design Lab

Typeset by Swordsmith Productions

The name "Hard Case Crime" and the Hard Case Crime logo
are trademarks of Winterfall LLC. Hard Case Crime books are
selected and edited by Charles Ardai.

Printed in the United States of America

Visit us on the web at www.HardCaseCrime.com

FOR SAUL DAVID

I have set my life upon a cast,
And I will stand the hazard of the die.
RICHARD III, V, 4

NO HOUSE LIMIT

Prologue

It started at exactly eleven minutes past three A.M. on Sunday when Bello made his first appearance in the pit, picked up a pair of dice, and asked that the house limit on bets be taken off. At first only the casino itself was involved, then the charged atmosphere, the fever and melancholy, spread like a plague to people staying under its roof. The ending came at exactly five twenty-three on Wednesday morning with the first cold, gray slabs of daylight.

So that was Zero: 3:11 A.M. Sunday morning.

But when was the real beginning? On what day, hour and moment was the decision made and the wheels set in motion? Or was there a definite time and place for it? It could have been a culmination of small events that at last erupted into the idea itself.

Take a day months ago when Nick Lotas and his two boys were unceremoniously ushered out of Rainbow's End, put in their black limousine, and told to start driving and not to stop until they were over the Nevada state line. Nick wouldn't have tried crashing any of the other front-line casinos because they are protected by the syndicate, which has made these places out-of-bounds for visiting hoodlums. But Joe Martin's Rainbow's End is a strictly independent operation. It figured Joe wouldn't be going by syndicate rules. He was, though. And Nick got the bounce.

That could have been the incident that started it, although nobody ever found out whether Nick Lotas had contributed to the money pool behind it or not. He *might* have. He could easily have chunked in as much as a hundred thousand toward the project.

Or was it another time, a different situation that was the germ that became an action? Morrie Stetten's wife came out from New Jersey to spend six weeks waiting for a divorce. Morrie's a big man in Jersey enterprises. He wanted his wife back. But she shacked up with some man in Las Vegas and wouldn't even answer his long distance calls. Morrie was told that the man was Joe Martin. It wasn't true, but he believed it.

Morrie could have kicked the whole thing off, not so much for the ten million dollars but for revenge.

Yet it is possible Morrie was no part of the venture. Ten million dollars is a lot of money and the plan could have begun in a penthouse in some big city, triggered by no incident at all, motivated by greed alone. Greed and envy and frustration, for Las Vegas is a walled city to outside hoodlums and they constantly look for a crack in the wall to slip through.

It is obvious now that they planned the invasion long and painstakingly. They knew it would call for tremendous financial backing and managed to raise almost half a million dollars. Once they had the money, they realized they needed one thing more—a front. A man who could walk into any casino without being questioned or suspected. So they obtained the greatest gambler of them all—Bello.

Bello was their first expense. You didn't buy a man like him cheap. He was to cost them seventy-five thousand dollars. Hot or cold. Which means: whether he won or lost. It was part of the bargain that he was not required to risk his own large fee. So what with other considerably smaller expenses, the show actually went on the floor with four hundred thousand dollars.

They were pitting that against ten million.

It was neither known nor suspected until just before Zero that Bello was the front man. Otherwise, the plan wasn't a very well kept secret. Word had leaked out weeks ago that something big was coming to town and that it would be directed at Joe Martin.

The town knew it, but the hapless patrons at Rainbow's End were totally unaware.

The First Day

One

One of the richest, most exclusive playlands on this earth is a strip of U.S. highway just outside Las Vegas, Nevada. A gaudy, sparkling honky-tonk avenue of gold, it glitters with giant neon signs, towering structures of stunning architecture, elaborate motels with shining blue swimming pools, and most impressive of all, dwarfing all the rest in undreamed of splendor, majestic monuments of luxury known as casino hotels. Flamingo, Thunderbird, El Rancho Vegas, Tropicana, Rainbow's End, Royal Nevada, The Sands, Riviera, Sahara....

As Joe Martin drove rapidly past the signs, the motels, the casinos, a desert wind licking at his face, he wondered if he'd be up to the big ordeal when it started. He knew it could start any time, even tonight. And he wondered if, in these days of his late thirties, he could cope with all the dirty pool they'd throw at him: the tricks and devices they'd use.

He slowed the car now, approaching his ten million because there it was, all in one piece—the biggest, gaudiest and best casino hotel on the whole Strip. The giant sign overhead was a fountain of color with the words:

JOE MARTIN'S
RAINBOW'S END

Below that, on the twinkling marquee, was the name of the thirty-thousand-dollar-a-week entertainer currently featured in his floor show.

Joe turned into the wide driveway, still gazing at the sign. Next week—would his name be blacked out at the top? Hell no, it won't be, he told himself. Am I getting soft in my old age? Not so you can notice it. When you're in this business, you've got to expect a rumble once in a while. I'll handle it. I'll send those creeps running so fast their fat little legs won't hold them. I was never afraid of anyone before, at least not afraid enough for it to matter —and it's the same now. The big trouble, of course, is the waiting; waiting for the first move. The suspense. Like those last minutes before your LST hits the beach. Once the mainline action begins, I'll know what to do and won't worry about it any more.

In the parking lot, he angled into the spot that was always reserved for him. It was six o'clock on a June afternoon, and there wasn't another parking space in sight. He switched off the ignition, climbed out of the white convertible, and headed for the casino.

He was just under six feet, his body lithe, stomach flat. He wore a crew haircut, and had a deeply tanned face that was hard, often inscrutably blank, sometimes mean. His gray eyes could cut into you, and usually did, but they could also shine warmly if he wanted to turn on charm. He seldom felt like it. He had authority, quiet-voiced dignity, and a big reputation. The women who could get close enough found his masculinity irresistibly attractive. But he wasn't easy to get close to, because whenever he *did* want a woman, he did the choosing. There was never any problem. At least there hadn't been until just recently.

The casino door was opened for him, and he stood just inside for a moment, bathing in the cool air conditioning. Although it was a full two hours before the floor show was scheduled to start, a line was already queuing up at the faraway dining room door for reservations. Here, close to where he was standing, the big, luxurious gambling pit was packed with people. A security man spotted him, and immediately made his way over, not to him, but within a radius of ten feet. He was under wraps again—protected from every and any conceivable angle. He started forward, and security men throughout the room kept an eye peeled in his direction. The old, familiar drone of stickmen was echoing from the four different active crap tables:

"Eight. Eight a number. Who wants odds on the hard way? Place your come and field bets. Here we go. Five. Five, eight the number. You're looking for an eight, sir. Eight'll do it." ("Come on, baby, sweat a little! Eighter-from-Decatur!") *"Six. The field loses. Eight the number. Let 'em roll. Seven. Seven, the loser. Next shooter. All bets down. The dice are coming out—do or don't come. Seven! Seven, the winner. Pay the front line. He's coming out again, the same lucky shooter."* ("Once more, dice, a natural!") *"Ee-o-leven! Pay the line...."*

The noise was rising to a steady roar: The crack of dice against the backboards, the multiple clang of nickel, dime, quarter, fifty-cent and dollar slot machines along the walls, the continuous chant of stickmen, voices pitched high to overcome the mounting babble of the customers. The blackjack tables, though, were silent: crowded to capacity with players seated in high chairs hunched over the green felt as green-visored dealers with green aprons and flat, bored faces dealt out the cards. But the roulette games in the corners behind them were audible—the click of the spinning wheel, and the voice of the croupier afterward, *"Seventeen, on the black";* and there was a periodic *whir* of the mixer machine behind the bar stirring up free drinks for wilted losers that would be delivered on nice, bright trays by pretty and shapely cocktail waitresses, wearing half boots and soft leather cowboy shirts.

From the elegant, leather-cushioned lounge that adjoined the casino, Joe faintly heard Mal Davis playing and singing popular songs. His eyes roved the pit for a few minutes, checking the action. The pit boss and floor manager both nodded, meaning that everything was normal. So he turned and moved into the lounge, heading for the piano.

He saw Mal now, singing as he played, wearing a white dinner jacket, a bow tie. He was slim, in his thirties—fairly rugged, with high cheekbones, blue eyes, and a short haircut. A man and two women were seated on three of the six stools around the piano. Mal had an infectious smile and he stopped singing and turned it on now as he saw Joe. The customers swung around to look at who could be important enough to make him stop in the middle of a song. If they didn't know, they quickly guessed. They always did. Joe looked the way people expected Joe Martin to look. And Mal cued them in fast.

"Hi, boss."

"Why'd you stop playing?"

"I've been keeping an eye out for you."

"Another advance on your salary?"

"No, I'm staying away from the tables this week."

For the benefit of the three customers, Joe parried with the usual joke: "Look, if you're not going to lose it back, how can I afford to pay you so much?"

After hearing this, people would say to one another privately: he thinks we think he is kidding, but he isn't. That's how they pay them those big salaries. The entertainers lose it back. Those casinos get their shows for practically nothing by the time it's over.

"She's here," Mal said.

Joe showed no expression. This is why I came over, he thought. Whenever she shows up, Mal always knows first. She likes the way he sings. Spends a lot of time at the piano. In fact, Mal was the one who convinced me I ought to give her a whirl. "For laughs," he had said, "besides, once you dig that body of hers, and the crazy way she walks, you'll be talking to yourself." And when that had failed to inspire Joe: "You'll never be able to make it in the hay with her, though. That chick is the original square."

"Boss, say something," Mal urged, grinning. "Talk to me."

Joe's face was still blank. "All right—she's here. Now you've told me." It was Mal's challenge three weeks ago that had mildly intrigued him. He'd never make it to bed with a girl like Sunny Guido. Well, so far he hadn't.

"Quit clowning," Mal said, "you like that doll."

Joe scowled. With customers present and listening, Mal was using his jaw too much. "Say where she'd be?"

Mal nodded. "One of the tables poolside."

Joe showed no interest whatsoever. Instead, to bring Mal down, punish him for running off at the mouth, he flipped a five-dollar chip over on the piano.

"Play something comical."

Then, to prove even further he had no intention of rushing out poolside to see anybody, he walked over and sat down at a nearby cocktail table. A waitress quickly brought him a glass of plain soda water, and he sat there with it, still angry. People said he was overly sensitive, too quick to explode. But the one thing he could live with least in this world was personal embarrassment; and he felt important enough not to have to tolerate it from anybody.

Mal Davis was singing the words of a love song against the background chant of stickmen saying: *"New shooter coming out. Do or don't come. All bets down, please. Who wants Ee-o- or any? Seven! Seven the big winner. Pay the line…"* while Joe sat frowning over his glass of undiluted soda water.

To a man at the bar who was watching Joe, and had been watching him for several days, taking shifts with others who had been hired by outside people, he seemed brooding—and somehow sick. That was good. It was something to report.

Two

In a gambling casino, the dice are extra large red celluloid cubes. The six sides of a die are each marked with a different number of white dots in such a manner that the sum of the dots on any two opposite sides will total seven. Dice—said to have been invented by Palamedes who taught the game to his countrymen during the siege of Troy—are the oldest known objects men have used for the purpose of gambling. They have been excavated from cities dating back to 1000 B.C.: made of ivory, knucklebones of sheep, carved from stone or metal. Pagan priests used them when they wished to ask the advice of their gods. The answer to any burning question of the hour lay in the way the numbers came up. There are men today who put that same trust in the extra large red celluloid cubes.

"…Nine, the winner, pay nine; same lucky shooter coming out again. Who wants odds on eleven?" ("Ee-o and any.") *"It's down, sir, eleven and craps; here we go—six. Six, the number. Who likes six the hard way?"* ("Twenty—hard way. Make it three and three, shooter!") *"Place your come and field bets.…Ten, the number is six.…"*

Joe was still sitting in the shadow of Mal's piano, and now, at last, he let himself think about Sunny Guido. The first time he saw her she was clad in a skintight white bathing suit and was lying face down so that the only visible part of her was the back of a rubber bathing cap, a slimly arched back and long, tawny legs, and he'd thought, idly, if any girl's face could equal this girl's figure, I'd trade the casino for her. And then she was on her back, looking up, as Mal introduced them: a saucy pug nose, a generous mouth, and wide green eyes that slanted up. He'd thought there couldn't be anything more perfect than this. But a few minutes later when she whipped off the cap and he saw her shining black hair in a poodle cut, she was even more beautiful. And she wasn't shy at all, the way he'd imagined schoolteachers. That's what Sunny Guido was—a grammar school teacher from San Francisco, down here for a free weekend she'd won on a TV giveaway show. Later, they'd sat at a poolside table, Mal still with them, munching chicken sandwiches, and she told them about herself: she came from a big family, her mother Irish, her father Italian; while in high school, she'd been awarded a scholarship that had enabled her to go on to teacher's college. After that, among the three of them they exhausted all the standard jokes about schoolteachers, none of them very original, but they'd laughed a lot, and Joe liked her. He wanted to go to bed with her, naturally, but he liked her beyond that. This was the unusual and disturbing part.

He'd spent most of that Saturday afternoon with her, then a few fleeting moments that night as she was leaving the dining room. She had thanked him for the ringside table. ("But that's part of your TV prize," he'd said), and told him how much she had enjoyed the show. So he asked her to have a drink with him, but she told him she didn't drink and he'd recovered, smiled and said, "I meant milk, of course—a drink of milk. I don't drink hard stuff, either. It's against the rules for a gambler." But the conversation began to pall as it always must sooner or later with campfire girls, and she'd bid him good night.

And on Sunday, when he finally got up at four in the afternoon, she'd already taken a Greyhound bus back to San Francisco.

She'd returned the following Saturday, at a time when he was busier than usual, and he wondered vaguely how she could afford it—now that it wasn't free any more. But he would have forgotten her existence that day except that she hovered around the gambling pit, playing a nickel slot machine, or just walking through, and he became aware of her eyes on him. There was something sexy about it, or at least he'd thought that then. So at four he asked if she wanted to see the sights, then drove her around in his car, ending up at Lake Mead. He took her for a speedboat ride, and she'd screamed like a delighted little girl. Then, in the middle of the lake, he'd cut the motor and made a pass at her right there in the bottom of the boat. She fought him desperately. The floor boards were flooded and her dress was soaked. It had ended in a state of chaotic clumsiness with him holding her pinned down until she agreed at least to give him one kiss. It was a maidenly kiss, and he'd released her. No apology, no words then; he couldn't wait to take the boat in and get her back to the casino and be rid of her. He might never have seen her after that, but a block before they reached Rainbow's End, with still not one word exchanged between them, she had looked over shyly and said:

"I'm sorry."

He'd laughed. *She* was sorry! He'd said: "I almost forgive you."

"I suppose I'm a prude."

"No, there are just some girls who don't care for that sort of thing in the bottom of a wet boat."

But why had she come back again last weekend, hanging around, haunting him: her eyes frightened, as if she were having a struggle of some kind with herself? He'd man-

aged to stay away from her; if she's working herself up
to something, he'd thought, let *her* make the advances.
His one concession was to walk her back to her room on
Saturday night. It was the only time they were alone. He
held her arm, guiding her, and felt the tenseness in her.
But when they reached the room door, she just turned
and looked up, as if she were terrified, and said:

"Good night, Joe."

And went in, closing the door. He'd shrugged.

He climbed to his feet now, moved into the pit, again
feeling the eyes of security men following him. So she's
back for the fourth time? Well, let's get it over with. I need
a little amusement. He walked outside to the pool area.

Now in the growing darkness of the summer night,
floodlights were on, and the pool was crowded with
swimmers. Sunny was seated at a table on the terrace,
sipping a tall lemonade. He sat down opposite her and
she looked up in half shock and surprise.

"Hi," he said.

"Hi."

"Looks like you can't stay away from this place."

She flushed. "I like it. As a matter of fact, I'm staying
ten days this time."

"Oh?"

She nodded. "School's out now."

"So you've got time on your hands?"

"Yes. I've been saving up for a vacation and, well, this
is as good a place to spend it as any."

He was conscious of her perfume now. It wasn't the
best, but it was effective. She was wearing a blue jersey
sweater, her breasts firm and sharp against it. There was
something wholesome about her. You didn't see this kind
of girl very often. Not in this town, at least. She was special. Well, that's why he was here. He knew all the other
variants of female.

"Were your fourth-graders sorry to bid you goodbye, teacher?"

"I don't think so." She paused. "Why do you make such a point of calling me 'teacher'?"

He shrugged. "Maybe it's because I didn't meet many of them when I was a kid. Didn't get very far in school."

She smiled. "One wouldn't know it."

He almost laughed. "That's a quaint way of saying it."

"What is?"

" 'One wouldn't know it.' Sort of formal."

"But *correct*."

"Oh, I grant you that."

"And I'm not as quaint as you think."

"Careful, teach—I remember you from someplace. Where was it—Lake Mead? Bottom of a wet boat?"

She was angry now. "Was *that* quaint?"

"Maybe not. But it brings me to something I want to ask. Aren't you just a little afraid to spend ten days here?"

"Why?"

"You figure it out."

She looked at him. "Big man of the world."

"I don't terrify you?"

"Not exactly. But I'm curious. What's it like being you?"

"Funny question. You want a funny answer?"

"No—seriously. What are your friends like? Close friends? And what do you do for—" she broke off.

"—*kicks*, isn't that what you were going to say?"

"What are your recreations?"

"You cleaned that up in a hurry."

"In other words you refuse to answer on the grounds that it's none of my business?"

Voice a trifle hard now, he told her: "A casino owner doesn't have time for friends—*or* recreations."

"What does a casino owner aim for—if anything?"

"To win—and keep winning."

"What about the future?"

"More of same."

"Isn't it a little lonely that way?"

"How can a man be lonely in a place that's always full of people?"

"Easy," she said.

"Well, let *me* worry about it."

"All right, Joe, I'm sorry. It's just that I've been thinking about you. Wondering about you."

"Is that why you came back?"

"I don't *know* why I came back." She caught her breath. "What do you think about *me?*"

"Nice. Period."

"That all?"

"The rest'll keep."

"You mean there's more to come?"

"That's up to you."

People were laughing. Men with strong physiques were doing fancy dives off the high board. Shapely girls in scanty bathing suits were watching, applauding, cheering them on. It was very hot and no one really noticed as stars filled the desert night.

"You're so cold," Sunny said, "that I find myself wondering if you're really human."

"Now you're getting there," he snapped, "what I really am is an animal. I bite, scratch and rut. So you'd better keep your distance."

There was sudden white anger on his face. And she said: "I didn't mean—"

But he was on his feet, kicking back the chair. "You heard me—stay here at Rainbow's End—but keep the hell away from me. That's fair warning."

"Joe—where are you going?"

"Where else? Back to my cage."

He moved away very fast.

Three

When a shooter throws out his very first roll, either seven or eleven will win—they are "naturals"; but should the numbers two, three or twelve turn up, he loses—they are "craps." Any other number that shows on the first roll is called a "point" (*"Six, six a point, do or don't, will he or won't he?"*) which must occur again before seven in order to win. After once making a "point," no other numbers (such as two, three, twelve or eleven) can interfere but the seven. If seven is thrown before making the "point," he loses the dice, which are given to the next player, in clockwise rotation.

Now, a few minutes after midnight, the first floor show in the dining room was over, and so was Mal Davis' session at the lounge piano. A trio, which—as prices go—was a much cheaper act, had taken over in his stead. And at the other side of the room, the buffet supper counter was open, dispensing smoked turkey and other edibles. Mal was seated at the far corner of the bar among the ten showgirls who had come off stage still in make-up. The contracts that paid them each a hundred dollars a week stipulated that in order to "dress the room up," they had to appear in the casino among the customers. So they always sat over here in a group. Yet, strangely, and to some of the girls disappointingly, they weren't often sought out. Statistics had long ago proved that for a male the attraction of a dice table was greater than that of sex.

Not that the girls didn't often have some stray Lothario, or stage-door Johnny buzzing around them; they usually did. Tonight it was the General—or at least that's what he said he was. He was dressed like a millionaire playboy, slacks, tweed jacket, open-collar sports shirt, and expensive leather sandals. Mal had met him twice before and had always found him entertaining. Over six feet, broad-shouldered with a handsome young-old face, shiny, well-combed black hair, a square jaw and abounding energy, he overflowed with big-time conversation that never stopped. The incessant chatter was laced with humor, and punctuated every now and then by an impressive statement: "I'm thinking of moving here. It's a coming place. I've put fifty thousand in with a group that's going to build a casino." Or: "I'm going to see if I can get a license to start dog racing in Las Vegas. There ought to be a fortune in it. I used to raise greyhounds in Florida."

Mal Davis didn't know whether to believe him or not, but the General put on a good show, and with such a friendly and good-humored flourish that he was constantly fascinated. The General claimed that he was here in town with his daughter and his mistress, and each girl was nineteen years of age, a circumstance that both amused and pleased him. Mal had met the daughter a few nights ago. She was nineteen and *looked* it, shy, naive, well-brought-up, on vacation from a college in the East. She seemed overwhelmed with her parent, but tried not to show it; she did her best to appear as madcap as he, but after drinking three champagne cocktails became ill and sleepy and excused herself to go back to the room. The General had looked after her sadly and said: "I really have to take care of that girl, now that her mother's dead." The nineteen-year-old mistress, if one really existed, Mal had yet to meet.

Right now the General was walking up and down, talking to the girls, making jokes; and he had insisted on buying everybody drinks, which reminded Mal of an incident that had occurred the last time he had been with him. The older man had been drinking double shots of whisky with no chaser and they were telling on him. Mal had had a feeling he didn't really know what he was doing, so had suggested that he try a single shot mixed with water and soda. "That way you'll last longer," he had explained. "I like to hear you talk, and I don't want you to pass out on me." The General had cheerfully followed the advice, *did* last longer, and tonight was holding a mixed drink. Which only meant he hadn't been an experienced drinker. To drink slowly and somewhat mildly was something you told to an eighteen-year-old, not to a mature man. And Mal didn't know why he was here tonight mingling with the girls. If he really had a young mistress, his interest couldn't be more than superficial.

"I'm going to speak to Joe about rearranging the show," the General was saying; "There's no reason he can't give each of you—maybe on alternating nights—a two- or three-minute solo of some kind to demonstrate what you can do."

The chorus girls, their faces glowing with heavy pancake make-up, and exaggerated dark green eye-shadow, listened skeptically. Mal felt they needed all that make-up to achieve the seductive, stunning effect they were supposed to have without it. Eight of them were medium tall, two were little ponies, all of them had ample breasts and good bodies, yet they were just passably pretty, and seemed somehow countrified and scared, as though they didn't belong in show business. It was an impression you got even when you saw them on stage.

"There are the happy, corn-fed future mothers of America," somebody had told Mal. "They're young, and having a fling at trying to become Marilyn Monroes. But inside of two years they'll all be married and settled down." And Mal, knowing these kids even better than his friend, had to agree.

"I'm serious!" the General insisted. "If you don't think so, I'll call him over here right now."

"No, *don't*," one of the ponies begged. "He'll say we put you up to it."

"All right," the General agreed. "But I'll speak to him first thing in the morning."

A long-legged, muddy blonde named Kate (who, nurturing a dream of becoming a musical comedy star, had given herself the professional name of "Kiki") was seated next to Mal, a spot she reserved for herself whenever he joined them. She was garbed in flats, black matador pants that were tight across the hips, and a red midriff blouse; her hair, worn in a horsetail, was tied with a red scarf. She was pleasant, and more sexy than the others, but she'd never make it to the musical comedy stage; and at the moment he'd have been happier with her if she washed off the grotesque make-up.

"Who is this crazy character?" she said, indicating the General.

"He's a nice guy, Kiki," Mal told her. "Harmless."

A few minutes later the General was whispering in her ear. After that, he whispered into each girl's ear, one by one. Mal was puzzled.

"What's the pitch, Kiki?" he asked.

"He wants to go to bed with somebody."

"You're kidding!"

"No."

"Then *he* must be. That's the type of joke he thinks is funny."

Kiki wasn't convinced. "Honey, soon as the second show is over and I'm free—why don't we go out somewhere?"

"All right with me," Mal told her, "only be sure you wash all that make-up off."

"Oh, Mal, why?" she complained. "It makes you seem more glamorous if they see you out with a showgirl."

He felt this was asinine, typical amateur showgirl thinking. He said: "According to *your* standards, I'm ten times as glamorous as you are. Now are you going to clean up or not?"

"All right, Mal, don't get sore."

A few minutes later she and the other girls headed for the backstage dressing room. It was time to get ready for the second floor show.

Four

Except for silver dollars, you do not play at any of the tables with actual money. The money is exchanged for chips which are made of a pressed rubber as hard as wood, and are very light. A piece of paper pasted in the center of the disc-shaped chip bears the name of the casino, and the worth of the tab: $5, $25, $50 or $100, a different color for each denomination; an invisible indigo dye is impregnated into each one, which discourages counterfeiting. The chips are interchangeable from one casino to another, and are accepted in stores, markets, restaurants, barber shops and garages. They are, in fact, a legal tender in Las Vegas, on an even par with U.S. currency.

Joe was holding a ten dollar chip in his hand, examining it against the overhead light. With him was Sprig, his top security man, and Clarence Henry, the floor manager now on duty. They were in Joe's small but elaborate, leather-encased office. It was well past midnight now, and the gambling pit just beyond the paneled door was crowded almost to capacity.

"It's a phony all right," Sprig said.

Joe was frowning. "No trace-back at all?"

Clarence Henry shook his head. He was a man in his forties; neat, mild-looking, wearing glasses, he could have passed for a small business man from the Midwest. "We found them in the counting room."

"An even dozen," Sprig said. He was tall, lean, gaunt-faced and blond. He was not only an experienced investigator, but one of the toughest men alive.

"I've alerted the tables," Clarence Henry went on, "the boys are watching for them now."

Joe took the chip back. "What worries me most is that it's so good. An almost exact duplicate of ours."

"I've doubled security," Sprig reported.

Joe looked at him thoughtfully. "Can you triple it?"

Sprig asked: "You think it's that serious?"

Counterfeiters made forays against them every now and then, but the danger of being detected was so great, it was usually a hit-and-run operation that never netted them enough for the casino to become alarmed. Yet Joe was now showing alarm. He looked at his two employees.

"I think it's started." He flipped the chip up, caught it. "With a ten dollar chip—or rather, twelve of them."

Sprig said: "I didn't expect them to go this route."

"They won't," Joe told him, "it's a diversion. They'll play around with this for a while, then hit somewhere else. I'm not sure, but I think all hell could break loose tonight."

Sprig whistled. "I'll call my outside people. Security'll be tripled inside of an hour or two."

Joe nodded. "Hop to it."

As Sprig walked out the door, the telephone rang. It didn't ring in here unless it was something important and the operator knew the person calling. Clarence Henry waited while Joe picked up the receiver.

"Yeah?" Joe's face was impassive as he heard the message; and he hung up without making any reply. He looked at Clarence.

"Guess who just checked in to one of our best cottages?"

"I couldn't," Clarence said.

"Bello."

"Well, he isn't—he couldn't be tied up with—"

"Hell, he couldn't!" Joe snorted. "He's a professional gambler. He doesn't care whose money he uses. Maybe they aren't even telling him. They could say it was a group of prosperous grape growers who want to have a fling!"

"But—"

"The *timing*," Joe said, "this isn't just a guess. Anyway, he's never stayed here before. Avoided me like a plague on all his other visits because I'm outside the syndicate and the boys in the syndicate are his buddies. Checking in here is the same as making a formal announcement that hostilities are about to commence."

Clarence Henry shook his head grievously. "I sure hope you're wrong." He just stood and looked at the boss, and then when time and silence seemed to be hanging too heavily between them, removed his glasses and polished them—just to be doing something. Joe had begun to pace. At last he turned to the floor manager.

"Well, what are you standing here for? Get back on the floor!"

"I wanted to ask you about the girl—Miss Guido."

Joe was in a foul mood. "What about her?"

"Been trying to see you since early tonight."

And he'd refused to see her.

"Where is she?"

"Waiting in the lobby."

"All right, send her in. I'm just in the mood for it. I

told her to stay away, but she apparently doesn't want to. So I'll fix her wagon good."

"She'll be stopped at the door."

Joe exploded. "So tell the guard it's all right to let her come in."

"Okay, Joe."

Clarence Henry left, and Joe picked up the phony ten dollar chip and looked at it. He was still examining it when the door opened and Sunny poked her head in. Then she moved toward him quickly.

"Joe, I didn't mean it the way it sounded!"

"Mean what?"

"I wasn't trying to hurt you!"

"Nobody hurts me."

"Why are you so nasty?"

"I'm not nasty, Wop."

Tears sprang into her eyes. And even in his agitated state, the tears got him. Facing her, seeing her, was confusing the contempt he felt.

"You need to talk to someone," she was saying, "*everybody* does, even kings and presidents. Talk in a way that you don't talk to other people."

He wanted to laugh; she was pitching pretty good. But he didn't even smile. "*You* want to be the one I talk to?"

"I don't know if I do, Joe. I can't cope with some of the things you expect. Not as fast as you'd want me to. But don't shut me out of your life."

"Why not, Wop? I have no room for you."

"Make room, Animal!"

"You call me that again and I'll knock you down."

"Go ahead, Animal!"

He slapped her hard, and she fell back from the blow, then dropped to her knees, sobbing. He stared at her, unable to believe that he had done this. Then he hurried over and picked her up and held her against him while she cried.

"I'm sorry, Sunny."

She pulled away from him, started for the door. He caught her in two strides, swung her around. She looked up, her lip quivering.

"I told you I'm sorry! Don't make me get down on my knees and beg to you!"

"Let go of me!"

He jerked her into his arms, lifted her chin, and kissed her full on the lips. She struggled, pressing him back; and then the struggling stopped, and she was holding on to him for a moment. When the long kiss was over, she turned away and sat down on his white-leather divan. He followed, drawing her to her feet, and kissed her again, her neck this time, her ears, her hair, holding her very close to him. Then he held her out, his hands shaking, and said: "There's big things going on in the casino tonight. I've a lot to do. I'll see you later."

She looked at him, calmer now. "All right. Tomorrow. But don't think because we kissed like this—I mean, just don't think anything."

"I won't think anything." He said it almost gently.

This time she kissed him. Tenderly, lightly, yet with ardor. Then she left.

Five

Three men work on the roped-off house side of a dice table; the box man and two dealers. Directly opposite them, the stickman rakes in the dice after each roll. Players stand at the side and both ends of the rectangular table and the dice must be thrown against the farthest backboard. The green felt cloth the dice roll over is marked with white lines: first, the "pass line"—where you place your chips if you are going to bet on yourself or whoever is throwing; adjacent is the "no come line": should you be opposed to the shooter. Among other betting possibilities plainly marked are boxes where you can place an even money bet on either six or eight during a long series of rolls; and squares showing the "field" numbers: 2, 3, 4, 9, 10, 11 and 12—for side bets on a single roll.

It was after 2 A.M. Mal Davis had taken Kiki out on the town, and they were now in the Sahara; but the crowded gambling pit was exactly the same as the pit at Rainbow's End; the noises were the same, the dice chant was identical. The bar (at which they were seated) was several feet longer, but just the same except for the faces of the bartenders.

Mal ordered highballs, then told Kiki: "Maybe I'll do some drinking tonight."

"Got the blues, haven't you, Mal?"

"Do I give that impression?"

"You've been moody as hell. But why? You've got a beautiful Cad outside—"

"And a beautiful cat in here," he said, looking over at her. Her face was scrubbed clean now, and the only make-up she wore was orange lipstick.

"—and a heap of talent," she went on. "And a name for yourself. So what else is there?"

It struck him odd that he didn't know how to answer.

"I mean it," she insisted. "Once you're a success, what else is there?"

"A few little things," he said. "Odds and ends."

She was a nice enough kid, but totally stage-struck, and he had her catalogued: the girl who will do anything for a career. No amount of talking, reason or logic can sway her. He'd seen her many times, with many faces, but the basic material was always the same. She was the bright, eager chick with a blind, fanatical faith in herself; and she was determined that nothing, not even love, would ever stand in her way. She was on a crusade, waging a war for fame. If you realized that she would never make it, and tried to tell her so for her own good, she refused to believe it. Either it was sour grapes because she wouldn't give in; or if she had, you were trying to get rid of her. Besides, it was pretty obvious you were no judge of talent. New York and Hollywood is full of her, she is everywhere you turn, and when you have reached the ripe age of thirty-six, you have learned it is useless to try to warn her of the pitfalls. Because nothing can daunt her—nothing except time, years of batting her pretty head against too many disappointments, and her firm white fanny against too many mattresses.

"How long you been in Vegas, Mal?"

"Only a few weeks this time."

"I know that," she said, "but I mean—"

"Oh," he thought a moment. "My God, it's ten years! I've been coming back once or twice a year for ten years now."

Thinking about that only made him sadder, and he was sorry she had asked, because now he clearly remembered his first engagement here. It was *exactly* ten years ago. He had played a straight six weeks in a joint on the edge of town while waiting for a Nevada divorce from Nancy, and never saw her again after that; neither she nor little Mal, who was only a year and a half old then; Nancy had married a cattleman and moved to some remote hamlet in Montana. She'd been his first real love, and back in the days before he married her, when he was twenty-two (My God, was I *ever* that young?), it hadn't seemed to matter that she didn't dig his music too much. He was going to knock the world on its ear singlehanded while she stood by and watched. That was the year, the first year of their marriage, that he was so broke he had to take a job playing piano in a whorehouse in San Francisco to earn both of them enough to eat. Nancy couldn't understand it and said, "You can drive a taxi, can't you?" She couldn't see why a house of ill-fame needed piano music anyway. "What does it add?" And another thing she couldn't understand was how he could say any of those girls in there were nice. ("Well, basically nice, honey. Some of them are just kids, sixteen, seventeen.") He'd gotten an education there, and never once went to bed with any of them, though Nancy didn't believe that; and sometimes, thinking back, he'd decided he'd been crazy turning down all those free offers. But you grow up and one of the things you learn is to appreciate that which you have missed.

Kiki was saying: "I sure wish I knew what's bothering you."

"Life," he said. "Is that an answer?"

"What are you going to do—get mystic on me?"

He shrugged and tried asking himself what it was that was depressing him tonight. Then he thought: maybe it's the disappointment over that recording session in Los Angeles a few weeks ago. At the time, it'd meant everything to him: whether he progressed with his music and his career and maybe even ultimate stardom in his field, or whether he stood still. Though he wasn't exactly standing still. Two years ago, Vegas had paid him five hundred a week; today he was working for four—he was going down. An album of records of his own songs, if it caught on at all, could skyrocket him to a thousand a week or more and push him on his way. Harry Muller had been sure this was it. Mal was playing at a bistro on La Cienega and on the eve of his departure for Las Vegas, Harry had

taped the whole thing right there, crowd noises and all,
applause, chatter and waiters rattling dishes and drinks.
"A twelve-inch LP, both sides," Harry said. "All Mal Davis.
People can sit home and drink and listen to it without
paying the amusement tax. I'm flying it to New York, and
I'll have it sold to Victor, Decca, Columbia or somebody
inside of ten days."

Now it was twenty-five, maybe thirty days; after two
weeks, Mal had deliberately put it out of his mind, planning to let himself be surprised when Harry called him at
Rainbow's End with the good news. But there had been
no call, and his subconscious had been acutely, painfully
aware of that. Yes, that was enough to depress him. The
fact that Harry couldn't sell the session. The fact that at
the age of thirty-six he had not only stopped progressing,
but instead had begun to slip. Two more years and he'd
be like that trio that had once been world-famous and
was now playing little joints in the San Fernando Valley
and glad to get the hundred and a half a week that had to
feed the three of them.

He lifted his drink. "To oblivion."

Her answer was: "I just don't dig this kick you're on."

He ordered a drink for himself, but none for her, because her glass was still half full. He was getting ahead of
her now. She looked at him worriedly. After a few minutes,
he said:

"Let's go downtown tonight."

She made a face. "Why?" It was as if he had asked her
to go to Skid Row with him. "What's downtown?"

"What's here?"

"Everything. People. *Class.*"

He said: "I'm going. You coming along?"

"All right, honey, I'll humor you."

Downtown Las Vegas is roughly two and a half miles
from the Strip, and on a side street a couple of blocks

away from the main intersection they passed a large, dilapidated house with a sign on the front that read:

Night Sleepers - 50¢
Day Sleepers - 75¢

"We're still in time for the night rates," Kiki teased, "and for fifty cents what can you lose?" He smiled, and saw her glance at the dashboard clock. It was three-thirty. The hour reminded her of something unpleasant. "Want to know what it was the old gentleman really whispered in my ear?"

She was referring to the General. "What?" he asked.

"He said if I came to Bungalow 138 at exactly three-thirty, he'd give me five hundred dollars."

He glanced over and saw that she was telling the truth. "I'm sorry I said he was harmless. *I* thought he was." He felt as if the world was chipping away from him. He couldn't even judge people any more. Then he considered the value and valuelessness of sex. He'd slept with Kiki the first time they met, and neither of them attached any great importance to it. Yet tonight she had turned down five hundred dollars to be with him for nothing; and it wasn't love, or even the nearest thing to it.

They reached Fremont, the main street—a shimmering canyon of neon, the giant signs projecting the images of dice, race horses, ace-high card hands, and sparkling horseshoes. The lights danced, revolved, flashed on and off; and through the plate-glass windows of the gambling emporiums he saw that the tables were mobbed. This was the seedy crowd, many wearing dungarees and work clothes; the women seemed dowdy, and older, and the men somehow more forlorn, as if they didn't really expect to win anything.

Mal kept driving, looking for a place to park, and passed the small Western Union office that never closed and saw that it, too, was crowded—mostly with losers, people whose faces looked sick, or drawn, as they waited in line to hurry a message back to someone in civilization. *"Urgently need carfare home." "Wire a hundred dollars at once." "This is my third telegram to you. Am desperate. Must have money." "For the love of God, send money."* But some of the messages were just the reverse. Outgoing money orders in large amounts. A Western Union girl had once told Mal about people who wired their winnings home before they could lose it back again.

The whole downtown area was as light as day, crowded, buzzing, and he thought: here's where the average working man loses his pay; and here's where the fugitives come, the real lost ones who have burned their bridges and don't even know that local and Federal officers are everywhere, ready to pick them up. He finally found a parking space in front of the telephone office, half a block from Fremont.

As he and Kiki climbed from the car, he looked at the small building. It had ten private booths inside, and two special operators always on duty, and he realized that, like Western Union, this was also a crying room. For a great number of people were too frantic to send a telegram, and made their requests for money by the more immediate and personal means of the telephone. Every outgoing call from this building was long distance.

He and Kiki moved toward Fremont Street. It wasn't plush down here; but it was far from being a Skid Row. She was too snobbish; there was nothing wrong with the central part of town.

"Where are we going?" she asked.

He shrugged. "Who knows?"

Eventually, they found themselves in the big impressive Horseshoe Club. They went inside, and he pretended, for a while, to be interested in blackjack; she sat up at a table with him as he lost five straight hands. Then he fooled around with two different fifty-cent slot machines. But inevitably they migrated toward the big display that made this club so famous—the glass-enclosed million dollars.

There it was, held in suspension, enclosed in super thick glass, but very visible. One hundred ten thousand dollar bills. An exhibition that cost the owner of the Horseshoe Club forty-nine thousand dollars a year—the annual interest a bank would pay on a million dollars. There it was, all that money in plain view, but except for him and Kiki, not even the nickel slot machine players seemed to so much as glance at it. The lonely, isolated million dollars that nobody could touch.

He was looking at it when he heard the nearby voices. He caught the words "Rainbow's End," then "Bello," and began listening closely.

"The big man's going to lay down a siege, they say."

"Think the action'll start tonight?"

"He doesn't waste time once he hits town," the other man was saying.

Mal caught Kiki's arm. "Come on, we're heading back to Rainbow's End."

Six

In addition to the regular chips stacked on the business side of the table are three rows of blue, yellow and white chips, unmarked; they are special, kept in reserve and never used except for the rare times when the house limit is off for a very big gambler. The big gambler, his rating established, plays entirely on credit. If he asks for fifty thousand dollars, his I.O.U. for that amount is stuffed down the slot—where it drops into the iron strongbox below the table, and he is given the blue, yellow and white chips, which the pit boss marks by hand: yellow, *five hundred;* white, *one thousand;* blue, *five thousand.* Others who may be at a table where a giant operation is in progress keep risking silver dollars and five and twenty-five dollar chips, and are generally more concerned with their own luck than they are with the big action.

At the stroke of three o'clock in the morning, the casino was packed, the action heavy; there was the usual babble of voices, with the chant of stickmen rising above. But now, a short seven minutes later, there was a commotion in the gambling pit; it was mild at first, then seemed to grow into a frenzy of excitement, one person telling another, necks craning. At exactly eleven minutes after the hour, the voices died to what was almost a hush.

Someone commented about it later. At precisely *seven* minutes after the hour word seemed to reach everyone at once that he was coming in; and he made his actual appearance at *eleven* after—as if to spook the house, or create another legend about himself: a man who was already steeped in legend. Seven and eleven, the two magic numbers on dice.

As he made his way toward a crap table, players fell back, opening a path for him, giving him plenty of room. Coming from hard-losing customers intent only on recouping their losses, it was an unheard of gesture. It bespoke Bello's importance. And now people were flooding into the pit from all over the casino, and from outside as well, to catch a glimpse of the big man. Mal and Kiki were among them.

"Probably the most famous gambler in the world," Mal told her.

Kiki nodded. "I've never seen him before, have you?"

"Not until now."

Bello was in his early fifties, with coal-black hair, graying sideburns, full, heavy features and dark eyes. Though his nose was a trifle too large, if he smiled he might have been handsome; but he didn't, his face was inscrutable. He was dressed casually in a charcoal-black suit, with a white sports shirt, open at the collar. His cheeks were not only cleanly shaven, but wore the bloom of a good massage. His eyes were bright and clear, indicating he'd been getting a lot of sleep and perhaps vitamin health shots. A gambler like Bello went into training prior to a prolonged play at the tables, just as a prizefighter before a title bout.

An exquisite young girl was trailing one step behind him. She was small, just an inch or two over five feet, with large breasts and rounded hips that were accentuated in a dazzling white blue-sequined cocktail dress. Blue sandal straps crisscrossed on the calves of her delicate legs, looking sexy and contrasting with her angelic-waif face which was framed with curls of dark hair worn in a short bob. She couldn't have been more than twenty. But she was Bello's girl, part of his entourage. He was noted for his taste in young and beautiful women.

Mal whistled when he saw her, and Kiki poked her elbow into his ribs. "I'll kill you, hon'."

"Just looking," Mal said.

Bello had reached the table now and was offered a stool to sit on—a standard concession to big-time players, but he disdained it, and his girl with the angel-waif face took it instead. Bello scanned the faces on the house side of the table—stickman, moneyman, pit boss, croupier and two security agents. He was waiting for the offer to lift the house limits on bets. At last he said:

"Is Joe Martin here?"

"I'll get him, sir."

But Joe was already on his way over. He had deliberately waited a beat. On the house side of the table now, his eyes met Bello's.

"Something I can do for you?"

Bello scowled, he didn't like it. Joe knew damned well what it was he wanted, but he was going to make him ask.

"What is the house limit on a single bet?"

"Two hundred," Joe said.

Bello shrugged genially. "Can it be raised?"

"Why?" Joe asked, as if he didn't know the man, "you somebody special?"

"No, nobody special," Bello murmured. And now Joe felt the crowd's resentment toward him, but he went on coldly:

"If two hundred a shot isn't enough, why don't you go somewhere else?"

"You afraid of real action, Mr. Martin?"

"There's no action in the world I'm afraid of!"

"Then why be a piker?"

"You want my money," Joe said, "all right. You take it the hard way—just like anybody else."

Bello's face was slowly draining of color. He made a slight movement as if to turn and stalk out; and if that happened Joe knew the name "piker" would stick to him forever, probably destroy the casino in time. But, if Bello was being paid to stage a siege, he couldn't afford to leave. He would have to stay and accept Joe's terms no matter what they were.

Bello remained. The table had gone silent, the dice had stopped.

"What's the matter here?" Joe snapped. "Get going. Who's the next shooter?"

"*I'm* the next shooter," Bello said.

Joe's eyes flashed. "That's all I wanted to know. You're staying, after all?"

"Yes, I'm staying."

Joe nodded. "My apologies, Mr. Bello. Yes, I know who you are. And the limit *is* off to you, of course. You play it your way."

Bello didn't ask what the initial delay had been; he knew.

Professional gamblers have their own unbreakable rules, and Joe had no choice but to lift the limit for Bello. It was a matter of courtesy, just as accepting his I.O.U.'s would be. To violate this practice could have earned him a world-wide reputation as a skinflint who runs a hall strictly for small-time suckers.

Dice were pushed to Bello. He selected two of the several offered. The others were drawn back by the stick-man, and now the chant started. *"The dice are coming out. Brand-new shooter. All bets down. Who wants insurance against any craps? Get the odds on eleven!"*

The crowd of onlookers around the table was now three or four deep. But there were no new bets on Bello's first roll. Joe watched closely as he exchanged an I.O.U. for the special yellow, white and blue chips. He placed two white ones—two thousand dollars worth—on the no come line, then threw the dice against the far backboard of the table.

"Three craps—loser!"

But Bello hadn't lost, not on the no come line; he'd bet against himself on the first roll—a precaution against the possibility he had been given fixed dice. Now he reversed his bet, pushing the two white chips, plus the two he had won, over to the come line, and rolled again.

"Seven, winner! Pay the front line!"

Bello's two one-thousand dollar chips had grown to eight, and he left them all on the come line. Others around the table were plunging money in now, most of them following his action. Joe tried to watch all this without emotion; but couldn't. Even now, when it was just beginning, each roll of the dice was dramatic.

Bello's third roll was:

"Five, five a number."

The famed gambler showed no expression, but did not seem displeased. He took time out and carefully made place bets of one thousand dollars each on every number from four to ten except seven. If the five was a long time in appearing, he'd reap a harvest on any of these numbers that turned up outside of seven.

Neither a five nor a seven showed for the next twelve rolls, and Joe began to worry. The whole room was in an uproar now; people tried to fight their way in close to the main table. In the first twenty-five minutes, Bello was already burrowing into the till. The twenty-year old girl seated on the stool next to him yawned, stretched her pretty arms. No one crowded in too close to her. The rumor was that if a man even looked at her, Bello had people planted around who'd take care of him.

"Five—five the winner! Same lucky shooter coming out again!"

"Place bets off on the come-out," Bello said. The eight one-thousand dollar chips he had on the come line had grown to sixteen and he now removed all but two of them. He rolled again.

"Six—six a number!"

Joe watched, waiting for the first reverse to hit Bello. And he knew that no matter what happened, he'd be glued here from now on. The war had begun. Bello was fresh, fit. Joe hadn't slept more than four hours the night before. But as long as Bello stood here, so would he. It was a compulsion.

"Eight…eight, the number is six. Get your field bets down. Nine. Nine, the point is six…."

Seven

In a Las Vegas casino, the wheels never stop, the dice never rest. There are no windows in the vast, low-ceilinged room to inadvertently reveal whether it is daylight or nighttime, no telltale clocks on the walls to point out an hour. So it is never day or night or any particular hour or time. The action is incessant. In the gambling pit there is nowhere to rest—no place to sit except at a blackjack or roulette table. If you venture outside, there are no diversions other than on summer days when you can swim. But at night, except to see a floor show, there are only three things to do—as all of the comedians and M.C.'s playing here tell you: *two* of them are gambling and drinking.

It was going on 5 A.M. and Mal was seated at a table near the buffet counter with Kiki and one of the other showgirls—Georgette. They had found her at the bar, very drunk and crying bitterly. A tiny redhead, one of the two ponies in the chorus line, she had a sweet healthy face with just a trace of freckles that had influenced him to think of her as the clean-cut all-American ingenue. But a little while ago, at the bar, she had gone to pieces: into a complete, hysterical frenzy. Kiki and Mal had managed to get her over here for coffee and food before the scene became violent enough to cause serious attention.

Georgette wouldn't touch her food, but sipped at black coffee; and Mal, as he munched a turkey and cheese sandwich, looked over at the pit. The large crowd had thinned considerably, but there was heavy action at three of the crap tables, and the last word was that Bello was a

hundred thousand dollars ahead of the house. Mal half
listened to what was going on a few feet away in the pit:

*"Coming out, do or don't come....Eight, easy eight.
Eight a point....Four, eight a number."* ("Strip the board,
a thousand on each.") *"Six, hard way, six. Eight a number."*
("Hard eight. Four and four, shooter!") *"...Five, eight a
point. Two, snake eyes. Pay the field. Eight a number.
...Twelve. Pay that fertile field again. Eight a point...."*

Georgette pushed the coffee away. "I've had it," she
said, "had it, had it, had it, all the way up to here! I'm
leaving on the first bus East without even giving notice!
I'm through with Las Vegas, and all the phony-baloney
jerks that go with it—and I just thank God I caught myself in time! Oh, what a beautiful bitch *I* was growing to
be. Know where I'm headed? To Omaha. Dull, insipid,
respectable and decent Omaha, the city of squares; I'm
going to stay there for a month with my folks, sleeping in
the clean virgin bed I slept in when I was a sophomore in
high school; then I'm going back to the airlines where I
started in the first place and where I belong. A nice blue
uniform, and good pay, and respect. Goodbye to Las Vegas
for *this* redhead; goodbye and good riddance—to the
dirtiest town on the face of the earth! Or maybe I'm just
not tough enough. Though I *almost* was. Tonight I was
almost tough enough for Las Vegas."

"I wish I knew what the hell you are talking about,"
Mal said.

"Listen, Mal," Georgette answered, being in a particularly revealing mood, "every woman born is a bitch to one
degree or another; if they think they can get away with it,
they'll do everything a man will, and probably a lot more;
they're more insatiable, more corrupt and have far less
conscience than men. They're more human than men.
Actually, they have a secret contempt for most men—who
are bungling, or think they're Big Deals, or are just plain

stupid. When they go to bed with these oxen they take an objective, impersonal, clinical view of his animal satisfaction, but it's ten to one *they* haven't been satisfied. Because with women nothing beats love, and loving for love. If it isn't love it's no good. Never, no matter how good or how great it is, it isn't really any good unless it's love. But where is love—I mean *love*—any more in this world?"

"Must be some place," Mal said; but he honestly didn't know where. He had believed in love for a long time but had never found it the way he had dreamed it. Now at thirty-six he had given up. Infatuation and great emotion existed, but a lasting love—no.

"Georgette, what's *really* eating you?" Kiki asked.

Georgette was drunk enough to level with her. "For years, ever since I started working, I've sent money home to my folks once a week. They've grown to depend on it—for bills, for everyday living. Well, lately, in fact for a couple of months now, I've been gambling. I haven't sent anything home. Then tonight a guy offered me five hundred dollars if I'd show up at his room at a quarter after three."

"The General?"

Georgette nodded, her face breaking a little now. "It sounded so easy—so quick and easy. So quick and painless, and all I'd have to do afterward was blot it out of my mind. Five hundred dollars for something I sometimes do here and there for nothing. 'Baby,' I said to myself, 'wake up—it's just this once, and your folks'll be squared away again.' I suppose that isn't a very sad story as whore stories go, but anyway, I showed up, trembling like a fool, and so scared and ashamed I was going to run away, when all of a sudden the door opened. I hadn't even rung the bell, but he'd been waiting and saw me from the window. And the awful thing is, before I could say a word, he was pressing a bill into my hand and talking to me in a low voice, saying he just wanted to see if I'd show up."

Kiki asked: "You mean that's all there was to it?" She was skeptical.

Georgette took a bill from her purse, a fifty, and tossed it on the table; then began to cry again.

"It's more degrading than if I *had* gone inside. Don't you understand? He wanted the mental satisfaction of making a prostitute out of me. *Me*—the tomboy from Omaha who played sand-lot baseball until she was sixteen. Straight as a die, that girl; clean as soap, sweet as candy—if you even say 'Boo' to her she blushes."

"That son-of-a-bitch of a General," Mal said.

"I'm glad," Georgette told him. "Now I know how low it's possible to be, and I'll never get down that low again. I'm leaving forever. Nothing can stop me. My love games from here on will be strictly platonic, and for much bigger stakes. You meet more millionaires in airplanes than you do in Las Vegas, and nicer ones. And remember this as long as you live—I don't care who says otherwise, you can't beat decency. You can't beat being clean."

That's right, Mal thought; please, God, grant us a favor: put us all back in high school, and let us start again—clean; we who were so wise then and are so weary now.

The cocktail waitress appeared at the table and Georgette said: "Give me a triple C and C." When the girl was gone, she looked up, brushing at her tears. "I don't know what I'm crying about."

"I do," Mal said. "You're proving that what you said is wrong—women really *are* better than men. You're the living example."

She gazed at him and wanted to burst into tears all over again because he had said that. "What a great guy! What a great guy you are, Mal."

The waitress returned with a triple Canadian Club

mixed with soda, and Mal ordered drinks for himself and
Kiki, and when they too were delivered, the three of them
didn't say much. Georgette was relaxed now, and the drink
was relaxing her even more. Mal said that sometime when
he was flying to New York he hoped he would discover
that she was the hostess; but she told him she'd probably
be working for Pan Am on the L.A.-to-Honolulu hop. She
was getting sleepy. Mal glanced over at Kiki.

"Better take her to her room."

Kiki nodded. "Want me to come back?"

"The mood I'm in?" He indicated Georgette. "And
after all this?"

Kiki looked uneasy. It was to her credit, he thought,
that she hadn't told Georgette the General had also pro-
positioned *her*. But she probably would later, when
Georgette was too knocked out to give a damn. Kiki
helped the little redhead to her feet.

"See you tomorrow, Mal."

Mal said: "Good luck, Georgette," and started over to
the bar.

Eight

The security watch in any big gambling pit is airtight. In
addition to regular uniformed casino police, and teams of
deputy sheriffs from the county who constantly come and
go, there are top-level guards in plainclothes who are so
inconspicuous that even the other employees have diffi-
culty identifying them. Yet they are always on hand,
eagle-eyed, efficient. Their principal function is to protect
the place from armed robbery and they are trained to
sense such trouble before it can start. But the subsidiary
chores are what keep them busy: spotting known crimi-

nals, grifters, con men, card sharps, cold dice men, counterfeiters and even stray prostitutes and seeing to it that
the casino police roust them out. Or, if the case warrants
it, they turn the offender over to the sheriff, who forcibly
escorts him out of town. Each big gambling establishment
employs at least twelve of these well-paid undercover
men who work in shifts. Some are former city police
detectives; several are ex-agents of the F.B.I.

Sprig had taken over Joe's private office for the dura-
tion of the siege, and now at 5:20 A.M. was still on the
telephone trying to get more help. He had managed to
double the usual security watch, but was a long ways
from keeping his promise of tripling it. He'd stay at the
job, though; from now on he'd be on constant duty until
the tension eased, no matter how many days or nights it
might take.

The trouble was, he couldn't get the ace people he
knew from the other casinos. Joe was an individualist.
Years ago when he'd first come to this town after achieving
a reputation as the top G.I. gambler of the Armed Forces,
he'd consistently backed away from offers of the syndicate
to protect him. "Pay seven percent," he'd said, "for what?
I'll protect myself."

At the beginning, when he was operating a small-time
joint on the edge of town, the syndicate itself had tried to
break Joe. Six casino owners came in and bucked heads
with him over a dice table for five days and nights. Sprig
had only worked for Joe a few days at the time, but he'd
seen the whole thing. Joe didn't break easy, and that time
didn't break at all. The six men left the place with five-
days' growth of beard and minus enough money for Joe
to start work on his own Strip casino where from then on
he'd really bucked heads with them for every customer
that rolled into town.

They could have killed him. But the syndicate was

not made up of hoodlums. They were businessmen who had long ago voted that there would be no gangster-style violence in this town. Anyway, publicity of that nature would frighten people into staying home. This combine of men, moreover, was determined to keep hoodlums out. And Joe wasn't a hoodlum. He qualified as a gambler. No side lines or rackets. So they'd taken the beating he gave them and walked quietly away.

"All right, all right," Sprig was saying on the phone, "so you can't do it. That's all I wanted to know."

He hung up and referred to a list of names in front of him. The door opened and two uniformed casino police-men escorted in a pudgy, frightened man who was wearing horn-rimmed glasses. Clarence Henry followed them. He walked over to Sprig and dropped a handful of ten dollar chips on the desk.

Sprig picked one up. "The phonies?"

Clarence Henry indicated the pudgy man. "He was pushing them."

"Pushing what?" the customer wailed.

Sprig stood up, dwarfing the man in the glasses, and looking lean, his back like a ramrod. "Phony chips," he said.

"I got them right there at the table!"

"Oh, sure," said Sprig.

"But I *did,* I tell you! That big guy in the green apron —the one with the little mustache. He gave them to me for a hundred dollar bill."

Sprig's eyes met those of the floor manager, and Clarence Henry quickly left the room. It was possible the little man was telling the truth.

"What's your name?"

"Todd. Dwight Todd. I'm from Salt Lake City, just came down for the weekend. I'm in the realty business."

"You come here often, Mr. Todd?"

"Yes, sir. Why, I have a credit card."

"It's possible there's been some mistake."

"The chips looked all right to me."

"You mind being seated for a moment, sir?"

Dwight Todd sat down nervously, and Sprig nodded dismissal to the casino police. They were walking out the door when Clarence Henry returned. A six-foot mustached croupier was with him, carrying his apron in his hand.

"He was just going off duty," Clarence Henry explained.

Sprig looked right through the employee. "Carpenter. Ed Carpenter. That right?"

Carpenter nodded.

"Mr. Todd, you may go," Sprig said.

The pudgy customer jumped to his feet and hurried out.

Sprig kept staring at Carpenter now without saying another word. His eyes slowly melted him. The croupier began to fidget. Silence. A minute passed and Carpenter was shaking. The guilt was oozing out of him in great blobs of sweat. Sprig at last came around from behind the desk.

Carpenter began to babble: "What are you going to do?"

"How long you worked here?"

"One week."

Sprig nodded. "Picked you myself, didn't I?"

"No, it was—"

"I screen everybody."

"I don't remember seeing you."

"You're not supposed to see me," Sprig said, "or even know who I am. Baxter sent you, didn't he?"

"Yes, but he—he doesn't have anything to do with—"

"Who does then?"

"It was just some guy—I thought he was a counterfeiter. Didn't identify himself or anything. I just thought I could—"

"Split with him later?"

"Yeah, I just thought—"

"You don't know his name, or what he looks like?"

"Well—no."

You find dealers stealing from you. All you do is throw them out of the casino. They can go across the street and take another job. Then they're somebody else's worry, not yours. But Ed Carpenter was lying.

Sprig knocked him down; then calmly picked him up, holding him by the front of his shirt. He shoved him back against the wall and worked him over a little with his right. He had bony knuckles and Carpenter's flat, mustached face was splattered with blood.

"Please, for God's sake, *please!*"

Sprig shoved him into a chair. Carpenter was whimpering like a woman.

"Ready to have a little talk with me now?"

Carpenter looked up and his whole body quivered. "Listen. Listen, mister. Maybe you don't know which side your bread's buttered on. Maybe in a few days this place'll belong to somebody else—and you'll be out of a job if you—"

"That what they told you?"

"Maybe the new owners will join the syndicate." Carpenter was chattering. "The syndicate don't go in for this sort of—"

Sprig pulled him to his feet again.

"No—don't!" Carpenter flinched. Sprig was mad now, wanted to hit him again, but he didn't. He shoved him back into the chair.

Five minutes later he was on the telephone, saying: "That you, Bax? Listen, come on over here, will you? I want to talk to you about something. Yeah, very important." There was a long pause. Baxter was evidently leery about showing himself in Rainbow's End. He wasn't, though, after Sprig, in hushed tones, said: "All I can tell you over the telephone is that the roof is beginning to fall in over here. There may be some big changes…" He hung up, satisfied, and gazed at Carpenter who was bathing his cut face with a wet towel. "He'll be over."

Clarence Henry had gone back out on the floor and they were alone.

Carpenter gazed up at Sprig and didn't know what to think.

Nine

The croupiers, blackjack dealers, stickmen and money changers who handle thousands every hour make twenty dollars a day; but the pit boss, who is in charge of the whole operation, gets forty. A cocktail waitress, working in the pit where the gambling is done, averages, including tips, a hundred a week. None of them has very much sympathy for the big losers.

"*Acey-deucy, three craps, loser, line away.*" But Bello was betting with the house on the no come line and picked up five thousand on that roll. "*Six, six a number.*" Now he stripped the board, putting a thousand dollar chip on each number. "*Four…the number is six.*" His four bore fruit. He let it lay. "*Four right back.*" The fruit had ripened and he plucked it, leaving just one white chip on four. "*Five, the number is six!*"

It was 5:30 A.M. now. The big crowd had thinned some, and Mal was at the side of the table, watching with utter fascination. Now and then he glanced at Joe, and saw the strain on his face. Funny, sometimes it seemed that Mal was just about the only human being on earth Joe liked…or at least tolerated socially. Except for Sunny Guido, that is. But right now Joe wasn't even aware that

Mal was alive. Rumor had the last tally one hundred and sixty thousand to nothing in favor of the gentlemanly Bello, and everybody in the room was running a fever over it.

Everybody except something wiggly at Mal's left elbow. For several minutes, caught up in the heat of the dice game, he wasn't even vaguely aware of who or what it was. Then he looked over and saw her and she caught him full face and smiled open-mouthed and wet-lipped as if everybody here bored her except him. It was Bello's girl. Mal's face flushed. It'd been a long time since he was close to anyone this beautiful. He smiled back, his regular professional smile, and she was encouraged to flirt with her eyes. A moment later Mal saw Joe looking at him and imperceptibly saying "No!" Mal took the hint and moved away.

He'd had a drink at the bar a few minutes ago and intended now to head for his room, but he saw the General seated on a bar stool, his back turned. Mal moved up, took the stool beside him. The General was immediately aware of his presence, but remained staring emptily ahead, morosely, as if he was waiting for himself to drop dead. The bartender came over.

"Straight shot, with a chaser, and one for my friend here."

The General's head came up slightly, and he looked at Mal in the bar mirror.

"You were the one who touted me off straight shots."

"It's breaking dawn outside," Mal said, "a time of day when things are always more desperate."

"I'm leaving here today."

"Are you?" Mal said coldly. "Without even opening a track for dog racing?"

"That was just conversation."

"So was your being a General, wasn't it?"

"No, I'm a General." He took a wallet from his pocket, opened it and showed authentic identification. Mal gazed at it strangely. The drinks came, and the General put the wallet away again. "I couldn't stay here and go on looking them in the face."

"Them?" said Mal. "You mean Georgette?"

"Which one is Georgette?"

"The little redhead."

"She and the other three."

"How many did you proposition?"

"All of them."

"All of them?"

"When I checked in here, I rented an extra room. I just thought if something stray turned up, I might have use for it. Then tonight I had a big, wild whim; and I offered each of the ten showgirls five hundred dollars if she'd come there—setting a different time for each one."

"A real sense of humor," Mal said bitterly.

"It kicked back on me."

Mal asked: "What were you trying to prove?"

The General rubbed his hand down over his face. "How many beautiful bodies I could buy before I die. I'm fifty-eight years old—how much longer do I have?"

Mal had guessed him to be no more than fifty, if that.

"I've been strait-laced all my life. Career, promotion, raising a family, setting an example; playing military politics—holding it down to two martinis, mixing well, being upright, sober, intelligent—everything I was supposed to be. Then a year and a half ago my wife died. I grieved for six months, and I'd started dying, too. Then one day I looked in the mirror and it seemed to me I was thirty again. And what I thought was this: I can run wild for four or five more years before old age sets in—and I'm going to do every goddamn thing a man ever thought of doing!"

Mal was somehow touched. "Then you really *didn't* know how to drink when I suggested you mix it?"

"No, I didn't. I'd been going around for a year gulping down straight shots, and getting loaded. I've been living big, all right."

"Really having fun, huh?"

"Until tonight." His face darkened. "Tonight I went too far."

"Wouldn't be any good to apologize to the kids," Mal reflected.

"No, it'd just make it worse."

Mal ordered two more straight shots. It was past six, and undoubtedly broad daylight outside. He wanted to drink himself to oblivion and hit the sack; but now the General's problem weighed on him. He brooded over it for several minutes, then heard a soft, low voice say:

"Daddy, where have you been all night?"

The General turned on his stool; so did Mal, and saw that the girl who had called him "Daddy" was not his daughter. She was a tall, statuesque platinum blonde with golden skin, and garbed in a tight white knit dress. She was probably nineteen, all right, but a different, more seductive and sophisticated nineteen than his daughter. The hair was obviously a dye job, but it was flawless and stunning, and contrasted her shining dark eyes.

"I was over at The Tropicana gambling," the General lied.

"We looked everywhere for you, then turned in about midnight." She evidently referred to his daughter. "But when I woke up half an hour ago and saw you hadn't come to bed, I was worried; so I got dressed."

"She really looks after me," the General told Mal. Then he introduced her. "This is Cherry. It isn't really her name. I just call her that because she's a full-blooded Cherokee Indian."

"Hi, Cherry."

"Hi," she said, then looked at the General. "No use going to bed now, sweetie. Why don't you go back to the bungalow and shave, then put on your trunks. The sun'll be out in another hour, and we can go swimming."

"These Indians are very athletic," said the General.

"He's pretty athletic himself," Cherry told Mal, and smiled. She was obviously very fond of him.

"Okay, we swim," the General said. He climbed from the stool. "See you later, Mal."

"Sure. Glad I met you, Cherry."

They moved off together, and made a good-looking couple. Mal wondered how the General managed without sleep; then wondered about a lot of things, his mind getting hazy, and wandering. Life was so confusing. Was he sore at the General for what he had done to the four showgirls? Did he sympathize with Georgette? Who is wrong, who is right, and what the hell time is it?

"Give me one more straight shot," he told the bartender, "then I'm off and running—for the sack. It's been a big, big night."

"Seedy" Baxter (his real name was Cedric D. Baxter) was a small-time promoter who had been mixed up in many minor operations in town for years. Yet somehow he'd never been in any real trouble before. Now, in Joe Martin's private office, looking at Ed Carpenter's raw, beefy face, then at Sprig's smooth, expressionless one, he suspected that his time had come. Yet Sprig kept up the con—or was it his idea of a terrible joke? He was saying:

"You've really got something, Bax." Sprig was too polite to call him "Seedy," or was that part of the con? "New ownership will naturally call for new faces, and I want to be in on the ground floor. Like *you* are. Now tell me, who are we going to be working for?"

"I honest to God don't know," Baxter said, and his face indicated that he didn't. "I was just in charge of pushing the queer ten chips."

"Who hired you?"

"Some guy I've never seen before."

"Without a name?"

"What's a name? He was nobody, I could tell. I can always tell when a guy's important. He was strictly hired talent."

Sprig studied him a minute and decided he was telling the truth, because Baxter was smart enough to know no matter how Sprig stood, the truth was his only out.

"So you rounded up people to push the queer ten chips. Who'd you get—besides Carp here?"

Even Ed Carpenter blanched at the way Baxter blurted the names right out: "Fat Morgan—blackjack. Cooley, roulette. And Carp here." Seedy Baxter shrugged now. "I swear that's it. I did just lousy. You keep too tight a house. I promised them ten bucks for every chip they pushed plus an inside track when the new management takes over."

Sprig pushed a button and two plainclothes security men arrived moments later. He asked them to pick up Morgan and Cooley, and when they brought them in, said:

"Float these scum out of town."

That meant all four of them would be driven to the Nevada state line, in the middle of the desert, and be left to walk or hitchhike from there. They knew without anybody telling them it wouldn't be healthy to try to come back. There had been times when a floater *did* come back. Days later he was found dead in the desert sand twenty miles away. Sprig felt that under the circumstances, the penalty was merciful.

As the men were being taken out, Clarence Henry came in. His shift was almost over. He looked at the guilty employees, then asked:

"Shouldn't we tell Joe?"

Sprig shook his head. "Why bother him? I'm his nerve center now. Anyway, this is only one unit of them. There's something much bigger going on somewhere. I'm sure of it, but I don't know where to look."

"One unit of what?" Clarence Henry asked.

"Distractions and confusion to pull him away from the main-line action. Once you get a casino owner off balance, you really have him. No, don't tell Joe anything at all about this—unless he asks about the phony tens. He's survived this one; maybe I can spare him one or two more just like it."

Clarence Henry looked at him, then nodded. "You're a good man, Sprig."

Ten

In the hot summer day time you can cavort in the cool swimming pool for a while, lie on the blistering tile beside it and sun yourself for an hour or two, and then, if the notion strikes you, put on a short jacket, slip your feet into beach go-aheads, and saunter into the pit for a little gambling. For no matter how ornate the casino or how plush the fixtures, if you have money to risk, even damp bathing trunks will be looked upon with approval.

It was nearly 10 A.M. Bello was now almost three hundred thousand dollars into the house. Joe's face was chalky and showed strain; but Bello was as fit as he had been when he first walked up to the table seven hours ago. His girl (Bello called her "Dee") had ordered coffee; but she could not have ham and eggs brought to a crap table and had been complaining since seven o'clock that she was tired and hungry. If Bello heard her, he showed no sign.

He had not budged from the table for even so much as a short walk to the rest room.

"Four...four, a point..."

"Odds on the four," Bello said.

There were new stickmen, new croupiers, a different pit boss; Clarence Henry had been relieved by another floor manager, Si Collins. The players and customers who had watched all night left shortly after daybreak, and those who had slept through the big action were up now, crowding around—women garbed in high heels, bathing suit and house coat; men in denims and tee shirts.

Joe watched the continuous, changing action on the green felt cloth and seemed scarcely breathing. He had a throbbing headache and wished Bello would take his snot-nosed flirty little girlfriend to breakfast. Even a thirty-minute break would help refresh him.

Then, suddenly, his gaze was attracted to the registration desk at the far end of the casino. Sunny Guido was there. She wore a beige knit dress and small hat. Two suitcases were at her feet. The desk clerk was looking toward Joe, talking to Sunny, probably explaining to her what all the commotion was about at this hour of the morning.

Joe caught Bello's eye. "Coffee break?"

Bello looked back with no intention of agreeing, then saw something in Joe's face and nodded his head, a courtesy gesture. It was only then, as he started picking his chips off the table, that Bello glanced with annoyance at Dee who was overjoyed. Now she could have breakfast.

"Thirty minutes?" Bello asked Joe.

"All right," Joe said. "And we switch to number three table."

Bello half smiled. "New game, huh?"

"Maybe a change of luck."

Joe was off then, moving toward the registration desk.

Sunny was gazing up at him as he arrived, staring into his face. Joe indicated her baggage, said to the bellboy:

"Take them to the penthouse."

"Yes, sir."

"But Joe, I'm checking out."

The boy hesitated. "Get going," Joe told him. Then he looked at Sunny. "Why?"

She was at a loss, and still studying his drawn features. "A lot of reasons, Joe."

"Like what? Name one."

She looked around. "Not here."

"Come on."

He led her up to the second floor penthouse. It was his own private apartment, encased with picture windows over which heavy white drapes had been drawn to keep out the summer heat. The thick, expensive rug was white, too, and the furniture black in contrast. Everything was extremely modern, the king-size divan low, soft. The walls were adorned with splashy Parisian watercolors. The bellboy was leaving as they walked in.

While Sunny stood in the middle of the room looking around, Joe walked past her into the bathroom, poured cold water and doused his face. He put his hand at the back of his neck and rolled his head around. Then he took aspirins from the cabinet, washed down three of them.

"Order coffee sent up…poached eggs." He spoke from the bathroom.

"But, Joe—what am I doing here?"

"Just order the food," he said.

"But—!"

He closed the bathroom door, got out of his clothes fast and stepped into the shower. He turned it on cold and stood under the icy water for five minutes. Then he was out, drying himself, climbing into a robe. When he emerged, Sunny looked at him, startled.

"A change of clothes," he said, and started toward the closet. "You order the food?"

"Yes."

He stepped into the closet, put on fresh shorts and a pair of slacks, then came out, bare-waisted, while he hunted for a shirt.

"I don't know what you think you're doing, Joe!"

"Will you quit arguing with me?"

"I haven't had a chance to argue yet."

"I've got a head full of troubles."

"Yes, the desk clerk was telling me." She moved toward him. "But how do you think it looks—having my bags brought up here?"

"I won't be living here the next few days."

"That bellboy—"

"Who cares what a bellboy thinks?"

"I'm not staying. I'm leaving Las Vegas."

He swung toward her, the shirt he had selected to wear still in his hand. He was barefoot. "That's right—you were going to tell me why."

She gazed at him steadily. "Well, just because—I can't cope with you. I found that out last night."

"It was a pretty miserable night."

"What has that to do with me?"

"I didn't have anybody to talk to."

"In a casino full of people?" She was giving him back his own words.

He nodded. "In a casino full of people."

She was scared now. "Joe, don't talk this way."

"Why not? *You* did, didn't you? Last night in my office? Who started all this? I was kaput with you. You wanted to come back. All right, you're back—and you're not running out!"

"Yes, I am!"

He pulled her to him and she struggled. He kissed her anyway, then let her go.

"I'm not like you, Joe. I just can't—"

There was a knock on the door and she broke off. Neither of them spoke while the waiter pushed the food cart in, then arranged the plates.

"We rushed it as fast as we could, boss."

"Fine."

When the waiter closed the door, Joe poured coffee. He drank the first cup black, then put sugar and cream in the second one, and sat down and wolfed his food. She stood watching him.

"You need sleep!"

He nodded as he ate. "Yeah."

"The skin on your face is all pinched and—"

"Then why do you give me trouble?"

She thought for a moment, and then her eyes grew softer. "You mean you—*need* me?"

"Could use you," he grunted.

"*Use?*" She was confused again.

"Bello has a slave girl. Needs her like a hole in the head. But maybe she gives him—I don't know, a lift of some kind. Knowing that she's right there with him. He's had a lot of experience, knows all the little psychological devices that make the big difference in a showdown. That's what we're having here at Rainbow's End. A showdown."

He climbed to his feet, put on his shirt, started buttoning it.

"You need me," Sunny asked, "as a psychological device?"

"Maybe."

"From you that's a big concession."

"Do you accept?"

"There's something I don't understand. Why do *you*

have to stay there every minute he's playing? Why couldn't it be somebody else—one of your employees?"

"Lots of reasons—important reasons. There are constant decisions to be made—whether, for instance, to allow a certain kind of bet he might want. Only someone of equal experience and crap shooting stature can handle it. Trust a decision like that to the pit boss, or even the floor manager, and if they guess wrong, it can begin to cost me the whole casino. Besides—with an action like this where outside pressures are putting on the big show, maybe somebody's gotten to your pit boss. A real gambler is always alone. He can't trust anybody."

"I didn't realize—didn't know it was that bad. That serious."

"Sunny—stick around until it's over. Will you do that? I don't want you hanging by the dice table, the way Bello's girl does; but when I conk out for a while or—anything else, I'll know that you're somewhere within hollering distance."

She said: "Somebody to talk to the way you don't talk to other people?"

"You were right."

"I'm glad." She came close to him. "That's nice cologne."

He grinned. "*You* smell nice, too."

Now her face darkened. "I really can't cope with you! I'm afraid!"

"Don't be. I won't be much in a mood for making love while the siege is on. And after it's over, you can go if you want—run as fast as you can back to your schoolroom. But I want you here in the penthouse. I don't want to have to look for you all over the hotel area. Just pretend you belong here temporarily and don't let a bellboy with a dirty mind bother you."

He sat in a low chair, pulling on socks, then squeezing his feet into shoes.

She smiled down at him. "The part I like is—that you need me. It's hard to believe."

"I didn't say exactly that."

"It's close enough."

"Then you'll stay?"

"Yes."

He stood up and, touching her arms, felt goose pimples. She tilted her chin so he could reach her lips, and he did; and was very close to her. Then her chest was rising and falling, and he thought it was passion, but it wasn't, at least not that alone.

He was holding her at arm's length now. "Joe, promise me something."

"I promise."

"But you don't know what it is."

"How many guesses do I need?"

"And you promise?"

"Yes. If you'll take care of me."

"I'll take care of you!"

She felt safer now, and returned to his arms, kissing him.

"Frustrated schoolteacher—that's what I am! Twenty-four years old and still a—baby."

"How come? A beautiful woman like you—"

"You just don't know how some people are. I live with my family. A big family…strict Italian father. Strict? He's a tyrant! Treats me like I'm still twelve. Runs off every man that—oh, why go into it? It's a long, stupid thing that makes me sound stupid every time I try to explain it!"

"If he's so strict, how come he lets you visit Vegas?"

"He thinks I'm with my aunt in Utah."

"You got her wired to back up the story?"

Sunny nodded. "What was it I called you—an animal?"

"That's right."

"Maybe I'm the animal!" Then she amended: "But a religious one, and a *good* one and—" She suddenly laughed. "This is ridiculous! You practically kidnap me, move me into your apartment—and I'm standing here making excuses to *you!* How funny can the world get?"

He smiled, delighted with her, then looked at his watch. "I'm going back to the circus. Keep tabs on me, baby doll."

"I will."

"Don't run off or anything."

"I won't."

He kissed her gently on the forehead, and left.

Eleven

A Negro cannot get into any Las Vegas casino or club, big or small, on the plush Strip, nor in any of the grubby downtown area places. He is refused the right to gamble, drink or even linger in any of them unless he is an entertainer or a janitor. There was once an exception—the huge, lavish Moulin Rouge: first interracial hotel-casino in history. But it was not on the Strip, nor even in the crowded downtown section—it was across the railroad tracks, a half mile up a street called Bonanza Road. It featured three spectacular floor shows nightly—white and colored chorus girls mixed—but it didn't last very long; it closed. Now it is dark and empty.

It was 7 P.M. and night again (day really; this, the early evening, was the real beginning of the day) and Mal was back at the keyboard. The stools before him were filled. Sunny Guido occupied one of them. She was wearing an inexpensive black and silver cocktail dress, and was paying less attention to the music than to the number three crap table.

Joe was at the number three table. He looked wan from lack of sleep, his face lined. Bello stood opposite him, gaunt now, needing a shave, his bristly, snow-tipped whiskers untidy and aging him; but otherwise he was the same expressionless gambler who had started throwing dice sixteen hours ago. Rumor had floated over to the piano that he was half a million dollars ahead of the house. A few more hours of bad luck, and Joe could be in serious trouble. The tension of what was happening was all over the casino and in Sunny Guido's eyes.

Mal lifted his hands from the keys and asked his customers: "Any special song you'd like to hear?"

And somebody said—the way somebody almost always did, any time, anywhere you asked for requests:

"Yeah—play *My Melancholy Baby*."

Mal began to play it, and after one run-through, sang it, too; and was startled at a new feeling the old song had for him. Maybe because Bello's girl Dee suddenly emerged from the big crowd around the crap table, and walked past the piano slowly, looking at him, then searched for a nearby cocktail table. There wasn't any available, but Diane, the waitress, prevailed on a couple seated at a table for four to let her sit opposite them. They agreed and Dee sat down, looking up at the piano. She had evidently slept through the day, because she looked fresh, brand-new.

And Mal thought: Man, she's something! Like I mean something. A real fabulous little doll: high cheekboned face, those lips. What a gorgeous plaything she'd make! He concluded the song.

"Boogie," urged a tipsy lady customer, "play us some real lowdown dirty boogie."

That mood fitted Mal exactly. He started slow at first, no identifiable melody, but a mean repetitive beat; then he began working it up, wild and crazy, keeping the same

one-two obscene undercurrent. Gradually, melody frag-
ments filtered through, but the dominating theme was
the constant bass, like tom-toms, the tempo rising.

So far he'd made no vocal sound, but moved his head
with the music, and held his mouth tightly shut. Bringing
the tempo up even more now, he looked at his audience.
They were all with it, drawn into it, but the women more
than the men. Sunny Guido was trying to subdue her
emotion but the suggestion in the beat had reached her.
This was jazz—undisciplined, primitive and dirty. He saw
that Dee, too, was devoting herself to the growing frenzy
of notes. Bello's girl. Her eyes were wide, her face was
glowing, and she seemed almost afraid to absorb any more
of it; she was holding both hands tightly around her highball glass.

Hell, he thought, I haven't even started yet. You won't
really hear anything until *I'm* lost in it—way out; gone
with the wind in it—deaf, dumb and blind to everything
but the rock, the beat, the low screaming, the fast running, the hard breathing. I'll reach a peak so high, you
won't be able to stand it. I'll take you out of this world with
it. Listen, now, because I'm starting. Now I'm starting.
Like I mean, I'm starting! Let's rock it; man, let's go—
let's ride. Come on, faster, crazier, wilder. Listen to those
beat-up mixed-up notes!

He was with it now, losing his mind with it, oblivious
to everything else, and he began to scat-sing—jumbled,
unintelligible word-sounds that matched the notes, coaxed
the beat. Scat-song words that moaned low, whimpered,
sighed, shouted, cooed, purred. He worked it up, kept
the rhythm throbbing, increased the beat, and now began
to spiral toward a crescendo. Faster, faster: hold on, baby,
hold on tight, here we go; go now; go, go, go; rock with
me. Rock me hard. Harder, harder, harder. All the way to
Loveville. Lift me off this world. Give me that ecstasy.

Give it to me. *Now!* Oh, roll, roll, roll—oh, rock, rock, rock—*ohhh!*

When he stopped playing, he was drenched with sweat, and he realized that he had closed his eyes. It was a moment or two before he could climb back down to the piano. Then he was aware that people were applauding. The customers on the high stools before him, and almost everybody in the cocktail lounge who'd been within range of his voice.

Sunny Guido's face was drained of color.

When Mal turned to look at Dee, she was getting to her feet; she seemed nervous, and left without glancing back. So he didn't know whether the boogie had finally *really* gotten to her or not, and was disappointed. But a moment or two later, Diane came up to him.

"The young lady asked me to give you a request."

"You mean Dee?"

The waitress nodded. *"Meet Me in St. Louis."*

Mal was irritated. "In the first place I don't know that song. In the second place, she's already left." He indicated the table where Dee had been sitting.

Diane shrugged.

He began playing listlessly, vaguely upset—and then it suddenly hit him: way out on the north side of town there was a crummy little place called the St. Louis Club.

The song title was an invitation for a rendezvous.

Twelve

A constant and infallible percentage of every dollar that is put down on a gambling table goes to the house. It varies from hour to hour, and even from day to day, but by the end of a month reaches an average. With dice it is 7 1/2 percent, but on blackjack never less than 30 and often higher. Roulette rakes in anywhere from 40 to 70 percent profit for the house, and the slot machines from 40 to 80 percent, depending on how tightly the screw in the back of the one-armed bandit has been fixed.

Now, at 7:25 P.M., the noise in the heavily packed casino was growing into a roar; the room was so full, people could scarcely brush past one another; the maître d' at the dining room door, trying to take reservations for the first floor show, was issuing fruitless orders for help from casino police. White lights burned down on the green gaming tables. A hundred slot machines clanged.

Joe, standing on the house side of dice table number three, didn't know whether he could stay on his feet five minutes longer. His head hummed and ached; his eyes were hollow, red-rimmed; his lungs burned from breathing in nothing but solid blue cigarette smoke. Twice he'd asked that the air conditioning be stepped up, only to be told it was turned as far as it would go.

Bello was roughly five hundred and fifty thousand dollars into him, and riding high and mighty. Joe doubted that anything could make him break stride at a time like this, and Bello had to ask twice before Joe heard him correctly:

"Dinner break?"

Joe only nodded.

"One hour," Bello said.

Joe nodded again and left the table. He had to fight his way through the surrounding crowd, but a security man and his floor manager both reached him after only a few steps; and out of the corner of his eyes he saw Sunny get off her stool near the piano.

"Send me up a filet—rare. And some soup maybe. For two."

The floor manager nodded, and Joe made his way to

the penthouse staircase. He was halfway up the private entranceway when he heard noises at the bottom. Sunny was arguing with a casino guard. Joe called down to let her in.

In the penthouse, he tore off his coat and shirt and flopped on the king-size bed, lying motionless. Sunny came in two steps after him, then stood silently, not knowing what to do.

"Yes, get some sleep."

"I can't," he murmured. He was a man in torment. He rolled over on his back. "I'm dead for sleep, but I can't even close my eyes!"

She hurried into the bathroom, coming out with a wet cloth. She knelt on the bed and soothed his face, his neck and chest. He frightened her, because his muscles were taut, like stone; it was as if all the muscles had knotted permanently. Blood vessels throbbed in his neck.

"You can't go down there any more!"

"I have to."

"But you can't. You're having muscle spasms."

"Nerves, that's all."

"It could kill you."

"Good way to die."

"Don't talk like that."

"I just wish to Christ I could sleep."

"*Try* closing your eyes."

He only stared at the ceiling. She reached a finger over, shut one eyelid, then the other. They opened again. Now she closed them both, and laid the damp cloth over them. He lay very still, and then she saw his expanded chest sink a little, breath hissing out; the muscles showed a faint sign of untensing.

"Just be still," she said, "just be still, darling."

"Huh?"

"Don't talk; don't move."

"Know what you said?"

"You're falling asleep."

" 'Darling.' "

"Did I? Did I say that? That's funny."

"Good, though."

"Good and funny?"

"No, just good."

"Sleep now."

"Food's coming."

"I'll keep it warm. You can eat it later."

She was on the bed, kneeling over him, so close that she felt his heart give a sudden flutter. It alarmed her; she was terrified. Then the heartbeat was normal again, and he was slowly relaxing. She said a silent prayer. The cloth was still over his eyes, and she smiled at him, very gently. Now there was a knock at the door, and all her efforts were for nothing, because he jerked the cloth from his face and jumped to his feet. She stood, too.

"Joe, it's just the waiter."

"I'm starved."

"You were almost asleep."

The waiter rolled the dinner cart in.

"Set it up fast," Joe said.

"Yes, sir."

"But you musn't *eat* fast," Sunny said. "It won't do you any good if you do. Try to be calm while you eat."

"I'm calm."

"Your hands are shaking. Is that calm?"

"You notice everything, don't you?"

She nodded. "I'm trying to be a very efficient psychological device."

When the waiter was gone, they sat down at the table. Joe took three spoons of soup, then pushed the bowl away and pulled the blood-rare steak over in front of him. He had devoured half of it when he noticed she wasn't eating.

"What's the matter?"

"I'm too nervous to eat."

"*You're* nervous?" It struck him as funny. He almost laughed.

"Anyway, I hate rare meat."

"That's different. Throw it on the fire a while longer."

"No, I'll eat later."

He finished the steak, but didn't touch anything else: salad or vegetables. He drank two glasses of milk.

"How much time left?"

"Time?"

"One hour."

She looked at her watch. "You left the dice table about twenty-two minutes ago."

"Wake me up in thirty-five minutes." He rose, lit a cigarette, took two puffs, and put it out.

"You have to sleep longer than that!"

"Will you do as I ask? I can call the desk, have them ring me in thirty-five minutes."

"I'll get you up," she said.

He went to bed, crawled to the middle of it and lay down on his side. But a moment later he was on his back, staring at the ceiling again. She fetched the cloth and brought it over, but he grabbed it and threw it aside.

"Leave me alone."

"I'm trying to help."

"Then lie down at my side."

"What?"

"I'm not going to rape you."

"I didn't say—"

"Forget it! Will you just forget it?" He turned on his side again.

She gazed at him timidly. "How could I help by lying beside you?"

He was on his back once more, his muscles growing taut. "You couldn't."

"Then why'd you ask me to?"

"Will you please shut up?"

He kept staring at the ceiling. The blood vessels in his neck started throbbing again. She'd never seen anything like this and was very frightened. Presently she unzipped her dress and stepped out of it; she kicked off her high-heel shoes and stood there in a black slip. He hadn't even noticed.

She moved closer to the bed, then hesitated, trembling. "You wouldn't trick me, would you, Joe?"

"I'm full of tricks."

"I trust you."

"Go away and die," he said.

She crawled onto the bed and lay down a foot away from him. He saw her now, was aware of her, but was too disgusted to make any move; because it *wasn't* sex he had in mind and he felt she should have been smart enough to know. He was ashamed of the real reason: he wanted her close because it meant he was weak, and if he was weak Bello was surely going to get him. Bello, the front man for those who were out for his scalp. He couldn't afford to be weak: clinging to the symbol of a woman: succoring strength from the roots of creation.

"Turn out the lights, Sunny."

She got up, found the switch, and turned off all the lights.

"How many minutes now?"

"Maybe twenty-five," she said.

"Come back here."

She groped her way through the dark to the bed and this time he reached for her, pulled her over. She was trembling, but he paid no attention; with her head on his shoulder, one arm under her neck, he fell into a deep sleep.

Sunny heard his even breathing, and knew he was asleep. She tried to remain motionless and keep her mind blank. She was afraid to think or feel. But now Mal's low-down boogie music began to echo in her ears. She tried to shut it out and couldn't. The beat kept getting faster. She caught for her breath. The sounds in her head wouldn't stop. She wanted to scream but the boogie music wouldn't stop.

Suddenly she slipped away from Joe, jumped up and moved through the dark to the bathroom. Closing the door and turning on the light, she stripped off the rest of her clothes and turned on the shower.

By the time she got Joe up, she had zipped herself back into the beaded cocktail dress and adjusted her hair. But she was still very pale. He asked her:

"We on schedule?"

"Exactly."

He washed his face, put his shirt and jacket back on.

"Good luck this time," she said.

"I need it."

"Maybe I'll be good luck to you."

"Maybe you will at that."

"Do you feel better?"

"A little," he said.

"You *look* better."

He gazed at her now. "You don't. You look like hell."

"That's a nice thing to say to a lady."

"Like you've been through a wringer."

"*You* don't look very happy either, Joe."

"We'll have to do something about it."

"Will we?"

He nodded. "Later. Go eat your dinner now."

He hurried out.

She walked about the penthouse for several minutes, a queer, sickening churning in her stomach. Then she took off her clothes again, turned off the lights, and returned to the bed. She moved over to where he had been lying. The place was still warm from the heat of his body.

Thirteen

In the summer the temperature frequently reaches a hundred and twelve, hanging there for days, and the humid desert heat presses down on the city in heavy, suffocating layers so that you almost have to be indoors where there is air conditioning in order to breathe. All of the casinos and clubs and better motels and stores, even small grocery stores, have air conditioning installed. But there are cheap downtown hotels that don't have it; and whole blocks of small houses in poor residential districts that are also without it; and sleazy, rundown motels and single furnished rooms where divorcees with no money live for six weeks that don't have it. In midsummer in Las Vegas to be crazy with the heat is more than just a saying.

It was hot tonight as Mal drove with the top down, a hot wind whipping his face, and now that the temperature had started to rise, it would be baking hot tomorrow, so hot that even the pool wouldn't be any good; the pool would be a warm bath, and if you tried to lie on the tile beside it, you'd fry like an egg.

He didn't know why he was driving in this heat, going seventy and eighty over the dark, black highway, unless *he* was crazy with the heat. He was still "on" at Rainbow's End; he'd taken his usual break, but was supposed to be back at the keyboard in ten minutes, and certainly no longer than twenty. Yet this trip alone would consume at least twelve and a half minutes—one way.

Why was he making it? Dee had dined with Bello, then left the casino just a few minutes ago. Before walking out the door, she had turned and looked straight at him. If he'd stopped to think it over, he wouldn't have budged. There was too much danger involved. But he hadn't wanted to think.

Now he tried to remember exactly where to find the St. Louis Club. He'd only noticed it once or twice before in all the times he'd been here. He made two right turns, and finally saw the neon sign: "St. Louis Club." It was in a lonely stretch of road all by itself and looked like a made-over barn. It advertised dice, blackjack, faro, and The Big Wheel. He roared up, slammed on his brakes, and climbed out of the car. The Big Wheel, he thought, that's where the only thing you can bet on is a number— no red or black, odd or even; and the profit to the house is usually 80 percent or more.

It wasn't until he was at the front door that the real fear and excitement of finally being face to face with her came over him; he paused, lit a cigarette and forced himself to go inside. He moved automatically, awaiting developments, ready to react to them without a pre-rehearsed plan.

The place was low-ceilinged, dingy, with one crap table, five or six people hovering over it. There were two blackjack tables, neither one of them crowded, and a scattering of slot machines. The Big Wheel and the faro game were over in one corner, and doing no business at all. But what chilled Mal was that there was an upright piano at one side of the room with some poor eighty-eighter thumping his brains out at it, and singing off-key in a whisky voice. But for the grace of God, he thought; then he saw Dee—and his heart beat hard and hurt him.

He started toward her, but stopped quickly. She was in the company of a heavyset man with a face so hung-down and jaded, he had to be the owner of the place. You got so you could tell them at a glance. They were walking toward the crap table, and Mal saw that she was pretending she had come to gamble. It spelled trouble—if the club owner hadn't spotted her as belonging to Bello, he wouldn't have moved in like this.

Now Dee glanced over at him, her expression a warning. So he was right. He dropped his cigarette, stepped on it, and walked casually past them to the side of the dice table. He tossed a five dollar bill on the come line, and pulled back two five dollar chips when the shooter, who had been working for a point, immediately sevened out. Dee and the owner moved up to the end of the table, three feet away from Mal.

"Coming out now, new shooter, do or don't come…"

The dice were pushed to Mal. He placed one of the chips on the line and rolled.

"You understand," the owner was saying to Dee, "I'm not asking you to leave—I just don't think he'd approve of you being here. We're pretty far out, and there are a lot of stags who might make trouble for somebody as beautiful as you."

"Ee-o-leven, the winner. Pay the line. Same lucky shooter coming out again."

Mal let the ten ride, and saw Dee put down a twenty dollar bill. It was exchanged for chips, which she pushed over to the come line.

"I read a pamphlet about all the different gambling places in Las Vegas," she said to the owner, "and I made up my mind to visit each one of them. He's busy at present, and I have nothing else to do."

"Seven, the winner, pay the line. Same shooter coming out once more…"

"I'll say he's busy," the owner replied. "I hear he's a half a million winner at Rainbow's End right now."

"I don't know," Dee said. "I don't keep track. Tell me, how did you recognize me?"

"I saw you when Bello started playing there last night."

"Seven wins again! Pay the line!"

Mal dragged back his forty dollars' worth of chips. Having made three passes—for both himself and the other customers playing here—he started again with the five dollars. Dee had only been in for two of the throws, and had eighty dollars in chips on the come line, which she refused to pull back. She apparently had blind confidence in him because nobody expects to make the fourth pass.

"Six, six a point. Come and field bets. Hard way six…"

"Hard way six," Dee said, throwing down a ten. The odds against a hard six were four to one.

The owner, now very conscious of the way the dice were going, was unhappy. He must be on a hell of a short operation, Mal thought. It looks like practically anything can hurt him.

"Yes, I want to see all the sights," Dee continued.

"Five, six a point…"

"For instance, tomorrow I'm thinking of visiting Boulder Dam. Which road do you take to get there from Rainbow's End?"

The owner explained which was the best route.

"Four, six a point…"

"What's the best time to go—in the morning, when everybody else in Las Vegas is asleep?"

"Well, they have tours, you can go almost any time. They show you through the whole place."

"Nine, six a point…"

"Would about eleven o'clock in the morning be a good time?" She sneaked a look at Mal.

"Good as any."

"Ten, six a point…"

Mal gave her no acknowledgment.

"I think that'd be a good time," Dee said.

"Six—hard six. Three and three. Pay the lady with the hard six—and pay that lucky line."

Dee drew back her winnings, a hundred and sixty from the front line, and forty more for the hard six. "Well, all right, I'll be going now. Thank you, Mr.—"

"Saunders, Nick Saunders." Nick Saunders was frowning. He *was* hurt; she had picked up two hundred dollars in less than four minutes, and the other customers at the table were also fat.

Dee nodded, walked over to the cashier's cage, converted her chips into money, and left the place.

Mal stayed on, conscious that he was overdue at the piano but it would look too suspicious if he followed her out. He made two more passes with the dice. Nick Saunders shook his head sadly, and then when Mal finally sevened out, ending the streak, drifted away, seeming discouraged—not just with the hot lick Mal had had at the table, but life itself.

The Second Day

Fourteen

Las Vegas has the highest crime rate in the country. Its police force is therefore three times as large as any other community's the same size. Its ratio of suicides is the highest of any city in the entire world. The victims are mainly desolate go-brokes.

It was 3:23 A.M., which meant it was Monday morning now. But nobody thought of it that way. Joe didn't, and doubted whether anyone else in the casino regarded it as anything but Sunday night. The weekend trade had been waning ever since ten o'clock—people hitting the road for home: an unending line of headlights strung all across the desert. The teeming, boisterous, holiday atmosphere had departed with the crowd, and the people that were here now were grim, serious—flat, monotonous; the room was a counting house filled with dead-faced professionals.

"Eight…eight a point. Five, the point is eight…"

The roulette wheel had closed down. One blackjack table remained open, but the fat, yawning dealer had no takers. He stood idly sorting silver dollars. Number four dice table had folded at midnight, and now number three was covered. But one and two were getting heavy action.

"Eight the winner…pay the front line…"

Joe held his hand over his mouth and hoped that no one saw him gasp for a full breath of air. He couldn't get it. No use trying. How long had it been now since the last stop period? Seven or eight hours. He wasn't exactly sure. He had a raging headache and his body wouldn't stand much more of this without relief. Bello, the older man, seemed in much better shape. Dee had flitted in and out until midnight; but since that hour remained perched at the big man's side, her beautiful and insipid face a blank. She'd slept during the day and wasn't particularly tired.

Bello was now almost three-quarters of a million dollars ahead and the taste of victory had him charged up; but for the past few minutes a small-time professional had been annoying him. Joe knew his face, couldn't remember the name. He'd come in earlier, and stood back with the others when the table was thronged three deep; but he'd eventually wormed his way in closer, until he was now standing beside Bello, trying to get a word in now and then whenever there was the slightest lull. At last he said:

"I have a club of my own."

"Good for you," Bello remarked, wishing he'd either go away or shut up.

Then Joe noticed that Dee was staring at the stranger. He smiled and nodded at her, and Bello caught it.

"What's the name of the place?"

"St. Louis Club."

"It's a dump," Dee said.

"Sure would help me a lot if you'd show up there sometime," the man went on, as if he hadn't heard Dee, and unable to look at her now. "Why, it'd *make* the place if you'd play there."

Joe remembered the name now. Nick Saunders. Small-timer—hanging on by a thread.

"Or break it," Bello told him.

"Yeah," Saunders laughed hollowly, "or break it. I take that chance."

Bello turned completely away from him and fastened his eyes on Dee. She was squirming. Now he looked up at Joe.

"Shall we go back to our corners and come out again in an hour?"

Joe nodded, excited at the chance for a rest, but puzzled. Bello left the table, Dee following, and Nick Saunders looking after them. Joe started for his office, but wasn't halfway there before Sprig intercepted him. The tall, gaunt security man looked like a young, half starved, unshaven Abraham Lincoln now, big circles under his eyes, cheeks sunken. But he was alert, tense. He'd already heard that Bello was leaving the table.

"Why?" he asked Joe. "That's what I want to know. *Why?* He doesn't walk away when he's lumping it in the way he's been doing. Doesn't make sense."

"I think maybe his girl's been chippying."

Sprig thought for a moment. "Yeah. That'd do it."

"Find out."

Sprig nodded. "How long is the truce?"

"One hour."

He clapped Joe on the arm. "Sleep it up, kid; we're going to need you on that front line every minute that Bello's there."

Joe sensed trouble beyond Bello's crap shooting skill. "Funny stuff?"

"I get rumbles," Sprig told him, "but you leave that part of it to me."

He hurried away before Joe could ask anything else.

Up in the penthouse, he got just inside the door, then almost collapsed. Sunny was in bed asleep, but woke immediately. She was clad in nylon pajamas, buttoned high on the neck. Joe was standing in the middle of the floor, the door still open, his whole body shaking with fever. His legs wanted to buckle under him. Sunny ran to him and helped him to the bed.

"Lie down."

"Not yet."

She crossed back, closed the door, then faced him. "How long?"

"You're learning fast, aren't you? First thing you ask: 'How long.' " He sucked in his breath. "One hour."

She looked at the clock. "Until four-thirty. Can't you even sleep until daylight?"

"No. Get me a drink. There's a bottle in the cabinet."

She started for it, then stopped. Her body was ripe and visible in the pajamas. "You told me you didn't drink."

"I don't. Get the bottle."

She reached the cabinet, picked up the bottle. "Now you *really* worry me."

"You argue too much."

She fetched a small glass and poured whisky into it and handed it to him. He took it down straight, handed her back the glass.

"You have some."

"You know *I* don't drink."

"This is another world," he said. And he had a fit of the shakes again.

"You're sick!"

"Sunny, I don't know *what* I am. Let me sit here quietly for a moment. Collect myself. Have yourself a drink. Give me another one. And don't worry and cluck over me. Act like you think I'm a man."

"I know you're a man."

"No, you don't know that yet."

She flushed. "Please don't—those kind of remarks. All I meant to say is that you're not indestructible."

"Nobody is, pet."

"Pet?"

"The teacher has become the casino owner's pet." He took off his jacket, kicked out of his shoes. "Unbutton me."

She hesitated, then knelt on the floor and unbuttoned his shirt and helped him off with it.

"You haven't had your drink yet."

"Please don't make me take a drink."

"Won't kill you. Oh, I see. You're afraid. Your true feelings might emerge and become your undoing."

She drank from the bottle, immediately spit it up, ran to the bathroom, poured water and drank it; but she returned, resolutely, filled his small glass with a shot, drank it down, then washed water from the larger glass after it.

"Bravo," he said. "Now me."

She poured him a drink and he took it neat.

"Now you."

She drank again, the same way, then gave him another.

"Maybe if you're drunk enough, you'll sleep until daylight."

"Can't," he said.

He stood up, turned his back to her and removed his pants; then crawled into bed in his shorts.

"Now you. Come on, climb in."

She was terrified. "Will you sleep if I do?"

He grunted. "But get me up at four twenty-five."

He lay still, his back turned. She looked at him, then at the bottle and the glasses, and suddenly she poured herself another drink. Her throat already burned from the first two, but now she took down a double shot, washing water after it. He had heard all of this.

"Taking it for brave juice?"

"Yes."

"Enough—and you'll be really brave."

"Will I?" Her head had just begun to reel. She took one more, smaller drink, then returned the glasses to the bathroom. She gazed at herself in the mirror with interest.

"Talk to me," he said from the other room.

She kept regarding her reflection with wonderment. "What about?"

"Anything. I can't sleep."

She ran water, poured one more drink, gulped it, then moved into the room toward the bed—and suddenly leapt on it, playfully, and pulled him around on his back, and looked down at him in the lamplight—his strong face, the square-cut jaw, prominent cheekbones. She ran her hand through his short-cropped hair and blurted:

"How many men have you killed?"

He couldn't have been more stunned. "What?"

She was playful and serious and drunk and reckless and too conscious of his proximity to her.

"In the war you mean?"

"No, in Las Vegas. *Were* you in the war?"

"I'm in one now."

"The *real* war?"

"Yeah—I made a lot of money gambling in the real war. After it was over, I was with the occupation forces in Japan, and for a while there, I had Tokyo in the palm of my hand —had a piece of every undercover crap shooting joint in town."

"Were you an officer?"

"A buck private. But I had everything wired. Came back with enough money to open up here."

"This casino?"

"No. I had to work for that. The syndicate contributed it trying to bust me out of town in a series of big-time crap sessions."

He was getting sleepy now.

She said: "Every now and then I get glimpses of you— what your life's been like."

His eyes closed solidly.

"How many men have you killed in Las Vegas?"

"None."

"I mean—people who won't pay or—whatever different kinds of trouble you have."

"None, none, none—stop asking such stupid questions."

"But I want to know everything about you."

He was asleep now and she didn't know anything. Crap

games in occupied Tokyo. Were there people who were *born* to be gamblers? What kind of a breed of man is that? Then she looked at him—his chest bare, his stomach flat; and she lay down beside him, but couldn't be still. Her head buzzed with the whisky, and then it seemed to her that her body was buzzing, too. He was safely asleep, she knew that by now; he wouldn't awaken until she shook him or called him. She sat up and took off her pajama top, then lay back down looking at him from the distance of a foot, but gradually inching closer; and then she felt her breasts against his bare body which was very warm. She crushed in closer, then heard her own loud breathing.

Now she reached down and unknotted the string to the pajama bottoms, intending to go no further than that, but a full minute hadn't passed before she was wriggling, trying to pull them off. She got them below her hips, and now attempted with first one foot, then the other, to remove them from her legs. She wiggled and twisted far more than she had expected to, and the pajama bottoms were off of one leg when he half awakened.

"What are you doing?"

"You wanted me to sleep close to you, didn't you?" She was whispering, her breath labored.

"Mm huh."

"Well, that's what I'm doing."

She waited then, in silence, lying very still, her nude body pressed almost against his, and exhaustion closed over him; he felt back into a sound sleep—unaware of her nakedness. And now she did not move any more. Fear negated passion. She remained absolutely quiet, trying to think, trying to reason with herself: and fell asleep.

Fifteen

4:03 A.M.

Sprig rang the bell twice and just as Mal was calling out a muffled "Who is it?" unlocked the door with a pass key, barged into the room and switched on the lights. Mal sat up in bed, blinking at him.

"What the hell's going on?"

"It's about Joe." Sprig closed the door.

"Oh," Mal said. He reached for a cigarette.

"I had to wake up three other people before I could trace you down."

"It didn't occur to you to look for me here in my room?"

"You *weren't* here in your room, lover-boy."

Mal studied his face. "That crack supposed to mean something?"

"How was she?"

"Who?" Mal was getting mad now.

"The little gal who asks you to play *Meet Me in St. Louis,* then powders out before you have the chance."

Mal gaped at him. "So what?"

"So you took a ten-minute break and it lasted damn near an hour! What did Dee Scott say when you met her in the St. Louis Club, chum?"

"You're quite a detective, aren't you? Wake up the cock-tail waitress—"

"Quit wasting my time! You were there. I can verify it a half a dozen ways. Don't make me. Just tell me what little Dee had to say to you."

"Nothing."

"She want to see you again?"

"We didn't even talk."

"Level with me!"

"It's the truth!"

"You ever met her before, seen her before anywhere?"

"No."

"Then *why* didn't you talk?"

"She was recognized."

"Nick Saunders?"

"Yeah."

"Now you're making sense. So okay, you didn't talk, but she'll set up another meeting—some other way—"

"She tried to. But I'm not going."

"Where is it?"

"Boulder Dam—tomorrow morning at eleven."

"Perfect."

"What?" Mal asked.

"You're going to be there."

Mal shook his head. "Oh no; I figured it out last night when I got back to the casino. That chick's too rich for my blood. Why, I could get killed fooling around with her!"

"Bello doesn't kill people."

Mal looked up.

"Hires goons to rough them up, maybe—" Sprig went on, "but we'll screen you every inch of the way, give you protection. Because when you *do* meet her tomorrow, *he's* going to know about it."

Mal jumped up out of bed. "What are you guys trying to do to me?"

"He's jealous. She's the one thing that can get him off balance."

Mal pointed toward the casino. "Are you talking about that crap game in there?"

Sprig nodded.

"Well, I don't want any part of it—of Dee Scott—Bello—

or anybody else. I'm hired to play piano and sing songs, and that's it."

"Don't make me say how much we need this."

"Get somebody else."

"The little tramp doesn't go for anybody else. Never has, any place, until now. But she's on the make for you."

"I tell you, I don't want her!"

"That isn't the point."

Mal moved about the room. "All right—then here's the point: I'm too chicken. I don't want trouble with anybody. It's hard enough to get through life every day without going out and asking for—I don't know how you guys get the gall!"

"It's not 'us guys'—it's me. Joe won't know it and there's no need for him to."

Mal stared at him. "Really do your job, don't you?"

"I try."

"Loyal watchdog."

"Do it, Mal. A favor."

"No, I'm not part of your police force!"

Sprig sighed heavily, staring at him through his encircled, bloodshot eyes, then shrugged. "All right. I understand."

He started for the door, and Mal said: "Would *you* do it —situation reversed?"

Sprig gazed at him over his shoulder. "Hell, yes. In a minute."

"How long would I—" Mal could scarcely hear the sound of his own voice, "—have to hang around with her?"

Sprig turned, leaned against the door. "An hour, two— at the most. In some cocktail joint in Boulder City. Then you break it off—real definite. You just tell her the truth: you're too scared to play house with dynamite. And after that, stay away from her, ignore her, no matter what she does—particularly once you get back here. Because if you don't, then it *could* be trouble. Real trouble for you."

"Wish I had guts enough to do it."

"You have."

"I like Joe as much as anybody I know."

All Sprig said was: "So do I." Looking at him—tall, thin, worn out, Mal knew that he'd do it, he'd meet her.

"Sprig, when you get back to the casino, send me over a double CC, soda chaser, will you? And put in a nine o'clock call for this room. I want to have plenty of time to shower and have breakfast before I leave for Boulder Dam."

Sprig smiled wanly. "Wilco. You're a good guy, Mal."

"And just one thing more. Don't worry about me ever seeing her again after tomorrow. I'm getting too old to go chasing baubles and bangles like her."

Sprig nodded. "Okay. Some other time, kid. I'm on a treadmill."

The moment he closed the door, Mal wondered why he had agreed to go to Boulder Dam. And then he was scared. He *needed* that double CC.

Sixteen

4:47 A.M.

The telephone in the penthouse rang five times before Joe woke, groggily reached over, grabbed it and heard Sprig almost screaming at him: "Bello's been back at the table for nearly twenty minutes. Your money's running out faster than I've ever seen it! Joe, get yourself down here! This isn't like you!"

"Be right there," Joe said and hung up. He looked at the sleeping girl beside him and wanted to kick her the hell out of the bed; but didn't. He shook her roughly.

"Get up!" And then he groped toward the bathroom. Inside, he turned the shower on *cold* and stood under it.

Sunny still wasn't quite awake. The whisky had drugged her. She was trying to rouse herself. She heard the running water in the shower and Joe's voice calling above it: "Get me a pair of slacks—a polo shirt." The water stopped running. "Hurry!"

Obediently, she started to climb out of bed, and then quickly threw herself back in, pulling up the sheets. Joe's voice was still beating her:

"I trusted you to get me up! You promised. That's why you're here." He came out of the bathroom, wearing shorts. "Where's the—" and saw her in bed. "Oh, pardon me, if I've disturbed you. Go right back to sleep." Angrily, he started for the closet.

She remembered her pajama bottoms would be at the foot of the bed, under the covers, and started to fish for them with her toe—frantically; Joe stopped, looked at her, then put his hands on his hips. She tried even harder to retrieve the pajamas. Suddenly he moved to the bed and pulled off the covers.

"Joe, please! Please give me back—please!" She started crying.

He went to the foot of the bed, found her pajama bottoms, threw them to her; and then he came around to the side where she had been sleeping and discovered the top. He handed them to her. She put the pajamas on, staring up at him, her lips quivering.

"Come here," he said.

She shook her head. "I'm *so* ashamed!"

"I said come here." He lifted her up. She averted her face. "Now give me a kiss."

"No—I'm going to leave here. First plane."

He pulled her head around, kissed her on the lips. "Why?"

"Because it's all over now."

"What's over?"

"You see how I am, don't you? If I stay here—"

"Oh, terrible things will happen," he said. He started for the closet again.

"No, I'll get your clothes."

She raced ahead of him, almost tripping.

"Sunny."

"What?" She was taking down a pair of slacks.

"Don't go away."

"Why?" She gave him the trousers, and returned for a shirt.

"I'd miss you."

"I'm no good." She gave him the shirt. "I have some drinks—and don't even wake you up. And when you *do* wake up, you see me—" She started crying again.

He buttoned the shirt, sat down to slip into his shoes. "Next time I have a break from the dice table I won't sleep."

"But you need it!"

"I'll just talk. We'll talk about you, about me, about everything. We'll talk a blue streak." He rose. "Do you know that I feel better?"

"Do you?"

He gazed at her. "Sunny, you still crying?"

She looked up, wiping at the tears. Her breasts pushed the pajama top out.

"That's better," he said.

"I'm awful, aren't I?"

"No."

"Just a cheap Wop."

"Careful. *I* can call you that. But you can't. Anyway, you're Irish, too. What do they call the Irish?"

She was gazing at him. "Aren't you in a rush to get downstairs?"

"Did you hear Sprig yelling at me?"

"No. I don't even know who he is. But—*you're late.*"

"Just say you won't leave."

She turned away. "I have to think about it."

"I won't go downstairs until you say it."

She swung back, staring at him, and then the words fairly burst from her: "I won't leave."

She moved forward and they kissed. Then they looked at each other, and she said: "Suddenly I want to call you 'darling' again."

"Go ahead."

"Hello, darling."

"Hi, teacher."

"Joe, I feel absolutely *giddy!*"

"So do I."

"Did the drinks do that?"

"No. No whisky in the world is that good."

"You feel it, too?"

"Exhilarated."

"Even as tired as you are?"

"Even as tired as I am."

"You were very polite when you—when you pulled the covers off."

"You were very beautiful."

"You were gentlemanly. I appreciate it."

"You're very strange, Sunny."

"That's what I think about you."

"Maybe that's because we're not used to people like us. I mean, a professional gambler doesn't often meet a schoolteacher."

"And vice versa. So we're not really strange," she said, "just strange to each other. For instance, I wouldn't be strange at all to another schoolteacher."

"I hope you're not anything to another schoolteacher."

"You'd better go now!"

He shook his head. "I'm glued here."

She walked over and picked up his jacket. "I don't want you to lose money—have anything go wrong because of me. Later you'd say it was my fault, that I'd kept you from your business. I don't want you to say that."

"I won't."

"When there's time we *will* talk. All about everything. There's *so* much to talk about. I don't know you; you don't know me."

"Honey, I'll see you in the casino when you get up." He shouldered into the jacket. "Stay somewhere where I can see you."

"I'm going to get up *now*."

"No need of that."

"Think I could sleep feeling like this?"

He laughed, and was going to pull her into his arms when the telephone rang again. He looked at it, then headed for the door. "Tell Sprig I'm on my way down."

"All right, darling, I'll tell him. And good luck this session."

When he was gone, her arms felt empty. And she was *very* giddy.

Seventeen

Boulder Dam is thirty miles from Las Vegas, a drive of about forty minutes on the straight good two-lane highway. Just before you reach it, you pass through Boulder City, a quiet community of stone houses with green lawns and a block or two of shopping section that includes cocktail bars and restaurants. The dam itself, which is the biggest in the world, is seven hundred and thirty feet high and a thousand feet wide.

Mal lay in his room, thinking about it, worrying, and woke just before nine—in time to grab the phone when his call came and say "Thank you—I'm already up." He climbed out of bed, bleary-eyed from lack of sleep and turned off the cold air conditioning; then he showered and shaved. To him, nine o'clock was the crack of dawn, an unheard-of hour—and it'd be a whole, strange different world outside. Different people, different crap dealers, and a solemn unearthly quiet all around like Philadelphia on Sunday. Las Vegas on Monday was just as bad.

Still, he wasn't prepared for the blast of blinding sunlight that hit him when he opened the bungalow door; nor for the intensity of the dry, unbreathable heat. He was garbed only in tan slacks, a short-sleeved pongee sports shirt and a pair of loafers, but was overdressed. He moved quickly in the direction of the casino-hotel, and by the time he reached it was drenched with sweat, his face and neck burning from the rays of the broiling sun. He stepped inside, breathing deep of the cool, conditioned air. He mopped his face with a handkerchief, then looked around.

There were no more than fifty people in the pit, most of them gathered around the only crap table that was open: where the main line action was on. He saw Joe on one side of the table, Bello on the other. Dee was nowhere in sight. But Sunny Guido was seated at a nearby cocktail lounge table. She seemed fresh and trim, and kept glancing toward Joe.

Mal headed for the Coffee Shop. The small dining room was bright and cheery—with canary-yellow walls that had murals of cowboys, lariats and cactus; and young waitresses who wore crisply starched canary-yellow uniforms. He sat down, picked up the menu, then heard a voice say, "Mr. *Davis!*"

It was one of his regular customers at the piano—

a skinny, angular girl of indeterminate age somewhere
this side of twenty-five, who had bony arms and legs, and
couldn't wear clothes right no matter what she put on.
She had a pretty though somehow quaint face, and a mop
of absolutely white hair—the closest thing to an albino
he'd ever seen. Her skin was ghostly white, and her eyes, a
light brown, sometimes seemed pink. Yet the very oddity
made her seem cute. She was approaching the table, and
he was surprised to see her in the canary-yellow uniform.
He hadn't known she was a waitress here.

"What are you doing up at this hour?"

"Exploring the other side of the day," he said.

Her name was Cindy, but he called her Cottontop. The
reason he knew her name was that she was the only person
in Las Vegas who had asked him for his autograph. She
had sat in at his opening night session, and that was when
it happened. "Write 'To Cindy,' " she'd instructed. "That
makes it *personal.*" It wasn't because he played piano,
wrote songs or sang that she wanted his signature: he had
once made a brief appearance in a motion picture as a
piano player in a night club. He had been on the screen
for less than three minutes, but Cottontop remembered,
and recognized him. She had a photographic memory
and remembered everybody who had ever done anything
in a film.

"You didn't know I was a waitress, did you?"

"No."

"What *did* you think I was?"

"Honey, to tell you the truth, I didn't give it too much
thought."

"A divorcee maybe?"

"I didn't think about it."

"Somebody's wife?"

"No, you were around too often. Husbands and wives
leave after a couple of days. You didn't."

"A showgirl?"

A shill, he thought; if I thought about it at all, Cottontop, I thought you were probably a shill.

"I didn't have any idea what you were."

"Well, welcome aboard here in the Coffee Shop, sir."

He ordered orange juice, coffee, toast and ham and eggs. Cottontop brought the items one at a time. With the orange juice, she said: "Tell me again about Hollywood."

"I've already explained to you—there isn't much to tell."

"Is it glamorous?"

"No. They're fixing Hollywood Boulevard, though, in the hope that it'll look glamorous."

"Do a lot of stars go to the Brown Derby?"

"Yeah, quite a few."

With the coffee, she persisted: "Is Beverly Hills glamorous?"

"Well, sort of. Yeah—I guess it is."

"Do you see a lot of stars on the street?"

"No, not very many."

"If you went to Romanoff's you'd see them, wouldn't you?"

"Quite a few."

"Like Marlon Brando and Gregory Peck and Bing Crosby and Gary Cooper?"

"Yeah."

With the toast and jelly, she went on: "Do many of them go to Chasen's?"

He nodded. "A lot of them."

"It's Jimmy Stewart's favorite restaurant, isn't it?"

"I don't know. Better check *Photoplay*."

"Where do you *think* I checked?"

Then she brought the ham and eggs. "If I went to Hollywood, do you think I could get a job there?"

"You might. But there are a lot of girls in Hollywood— and almost all of them are looking for jobs."

"Oh, I mean in a place like Romanoff's."

"Romanoff's uses men waiters." He saw her eyes. "So does Chasen's, The Brown Derby, Encore and the Mocambo."

She was crestfallen. "Is that the truth?"

"Yep. Honey, you'll see more movie actors close up in Las Vegas than you will anywhere else in the world."

Cottontop thought it over. "Yes, I've seen a *lot* of them here. I have three autograph books all filled, and I'm working on my fourth. Mr. Davis, when you make another picture, please let me know so I can go see it. Just write me a card here at Rainbow's End. I'll be here. I'll probably be here forever."

He finished his breakfast, tipped her a dollar, and left.

A few moments later he groped his way through the sizzling heat to the parking lot, and once he was seated on the blistering leather upholstery in the white Cad, put the top up to protect himself from the sun.

He reached Boulder Dam a half an hour later, parked the car, then stood on the opposite side of the street from the shimmering mass of stopped-up water in the Colorado River where he could look over the stone embankment far down at the people moving around the bottom of the dry side of the dam. Now, here by the river, there was a riffle of breeze, and the weather was almost, but not quite, endurable.

He waited several minutes, watching everything and everyone, but it still wasn't eleven o'clock yet. He had managed to calm his emotions by a dull, flat inner certainty that Dee wouldn't show up. And even when he saw the sleek, blue Cad back into a parking space down the street, he was positive she couldn't be the driver. But she stepped from it, wearing a sleeveless yellow dress and bright toeless sandals, and started toward the dam.

He looked at her as she approached—the short-cut

black hair, her sad, angelic little face with the big eyes and the large mouth, and wondered why she had to be so dangerous to know. She saw him now and quickened her step.

They stood there just looking at one another for a moment, and there was something wondrous about it.

"Hi," he said.

"Hi."

"Want to see the dam?"

"Do you?"

"We're here," he said, "so we might as well."

"Why?"

"No reason, I guess."

"What I came here to see was you."

"You're seeing." He was hoping she'd be disillusioned, disenchanted: making it easier to break off with her.

She said: "And I like."

"You're a beautiful girl, Dee." It was an understatement.

"Let's go somewhere!"

He remembered Sprig's instructions. "A bar maybe? In Boulder City?"

"Fine!"

"My car or yours?"

"Let's take both of them."

"You mean—for a quick getaway, if necessary?"

"That's cruel."

He'd meant it to be cruel. He was building up for his explanation of why he wouldn't want to see her any more.

"All right, we'll take both of them. Must be at least two miles back to Boulder City."

"I'll follow you," she said.

"Good."

"Mal—" He turned back. "Don't look so awfully disgusted with me."

He peered at her. "What a thing to say!"

"You're not like last night at all."

"Dee, maybe I'm scared."

"You drive, I'll follow."

In Boulder City, they walked into two cocktail restaurants before the third one proved to be dark and moody enough. They sat at a secluded table back by the wall, with only a candle between them, making a tiny light. They hadn't spoken since leaving the dam, and now she said:

"I'm scared, too."

It startled him.

"He knows about last night," she went on.

"About me?"

"Not you—by name. But he suspects I went there to meet somebody."

It hadn't occurred to Mal she would be as frightened as he was; for a moment, it was something he didn't know how to cope with. Then he came right out with it:

"He's going to know about this meeting, too."

She almost blanched. "*Why?* I have his permission to go to Boulder Dam."

"Is this a dam?"

"We're being watched?"

He nodded.

"By whom? Somebody he's hired?"

And now he no longer had the courage to tell her the truth. "Yeah." Let it go at that.

"Oh, God, I'm sick of it!" she said. "I'm sick of this!"

"I don't think we should meet again." There! It was said.

"All right. And goodbye." Her eyes were wet.

He was uneasy. "Goodbye? This minute?"

"Run away. I can't, but you go ahead."

He was leaning forward. "*Why* can't you?"

"What do you want—the story of my life?"

"If you really want to go there's no way he can hold you."

"Where would I go? Back to dancing in a second-rate casino in Covington, Kentucky, where three-fourths of the girls are prostitutes on the side? Or to my family? My mother and father who live in the slums of Cincinnati? You'd love my father. Came home drunk one night and raped me. Listen, I met Mr. Bello in Covington. He gambled there. He wanted me. He was a gentleman. He had a lot to offer. A mink coat—clothes, a car—and even an ounce and a half of dignity. I went for it. My eyes were open. I'm not apologizing. But now I can't take it any more and I don't know how to get out. Not without giving it all back. Which means, I'd hit the road every other girl hits. Do you *really* think I'm beautiful?"

"Yes."

"So I'd get along—but *like that?* I've made the last deal for my body I'm ever going to make. The first deal and the last one. Now the thing is, I had to tell this to some-body. Anybody who'd listen. I heard you sing last night and watched your face and saw something in your eyes so I selected you. It's a very sad story, isn't it? You're moved, aren't you? Well, the story's over now, so you can go."

"What was it you saw in my eyes?"

"Never mind, I was mistaken."

"Tell me!"

"Sympathy," she said. "I thought you were the kind who'd *want* to help somebody in trouble. It was the trance the music put me in—I actually—for a crazy minute—thought you were somebody to turn to. So I was wrong." Now she examined his face. "What did *you* think my reason was? I wanted to make a pass at you? That I ar-ranged to meet you because I was looking for a quick lay somewhere? Oh, you were wrong, mister. We both were. Scratch it all out—it never happened."

"Dee, you're crying!"

"Yes, I'm crying. But it's dark in here, nobody'll see, not even his pet spy, whoever he is; nobody can see but you—and it doesn't matter to you."

Gazing at her intently, he felt challenged now.

"Anyway," she said, "I thought you were leaving?"

And he said: "I thought I was, too."

Eighteen

Shills are considered one of the lowest forms of casino humanity, yet are not only necessary, but must dress and seem to look like the well-to-do customers. During slow hours it is their duty to make a dead or a "cold" table come alive. They converge on it, one at a time, and start playing, using silver dollars that have been advanced to them by the house. At the end of a shift they return the money along with whatever they have won; it is impossible to hold out, as a croupier has kept a careful tally. When they have drawn legitimate players to the game, they drop out and are directed by a signal from the pit boss to a less prosperous area: a blackjack game that has dwindled to nothing, or an idle roulette wheel.

The usual wage of a shill is six dollars a day, and they do not have to be recruited. Every casino has a waiting list: men who have gone broke and for whatever reason can't return home eke out a bare existence at the work. Divorcees waiting out the six weeks augment their meager allowance. Off-duty waitresses find it a way to pick up extra money. They would be perfect decoys except that they are easily detected by the total lack of interest they show as they pretend to gamble.

It was noon now, a slow hour on an ordinarily slow day,

but the casino was gradually whipping up momentum: mostly because of the big game which was legend all over town. Spectators crowded in and some eventually drifted to the other tables to gamble. Number two table was packed, number three was getting a fair play and the croupiers had just taken the wraps off number four.

Shills in various parts of the room had their eyes on it, waiting for the signal to come over. Nobody likes to risk money in a cold, lonely place and they'd give it the push it needed—like a car with a faulty battery.

Joe stood across the main table from Bello, his shirt open at the throat. He had slipped into the office a while ago, long enough to shave; he operated on the theory that the owner of the place should always make a neat appearance. He was wan, gaunt, but Bello looked worse now. The grueling, unending hours were beginning to weigh on him. His dark eyes seemed sunken, and his face was covered with a heavy, black, gray-tipped beard. He looked around every now and then, as if wondering where Dee was.

Bello had passed the eight hundred thousand dollar mark during the early hours of the morning, but after Joe appeared, around 5 A.M., had tapered off and was now under seven hundred thousand winner: enough to quit and walk away with a fabulous coup. But he wasn't quitting, and Joe knew why. This was the big game of the big man's lifetime. And it wouldn't be *his* money, anyway, he'd get his fee, maybe a fat bonus—no more. The bulk of the winnings would belong to his backers. So he could *afford* to appear tremendous in the eyes of the public—a big winner, but playing for more. "Trying to win the cloth off the table."

The stickmen droned: *"Four…four a point…take the odds on four."* ("Come on, dice—how do ducks come to water—two by two!") *"Five, the number is four. Four a*

point, four will win it. Six, out of the field, the number is
four. The shooter must make a four. Seven! Seven, loser.
Line away. New shooter coming out...."

That chipped Bello down over ten thousand. Joe
glanced across the room at Sunny. She was at the same
cocktail table, glancing through the pages of a fashion
magazine. On a crazy impulse, he sent for a secretary.
"Have her bring a shorthand book."

The secretary arrived fifteen minutes later, and by that
time the whim had left Joe. He was about to dismiss her,
when he noticed the curious look on Bello's face—seeing
a woman with a shorthand book and a pencil on the house
side of the dice table. Joe was delighted. Hell, he thought,
it bothers him; and any little distraction counts right now.
It'll distract me to dictate, even haphazard, only a few
words at a time, but it'll worry him even more, wondering
what I'm doing.

So he kept the secretary, and whenever he had a
moment, leaned over and spoke a few words into her
ear—which she jotted down. The dictation was so spo-
radic it seemed as if he was making notes on Bello's play,
and the famous gambler frowned at this; his expression
made it appear as if Joe was committing some cardinal
discourtesy.

So he continued it. The girl was there nearly forty
minutes, and he would have dictated even longer, but
something began to bother and alarm him. The drone of
the stickman had changed, the calls were different. It was
as if a river flowing at a certain speed had suddenly
started moving with a roar. *"Seven, seven the winner! Pay*
the board. Coming out again. Ee-o-leven—lucky eleven.
Pay the board! Here we go once again, all bets down!
Who wants the odds on craps? Seven! Seven again!" In
between hot surges like these a number would be thrown
—always a six or an eight—and it would seven out the

very next throw. Then the sevens and elevens would start again. It was a feat mathematically incredible for regular playing dice.

Joe studied Bello, glaring at him. But the gambler was so swept up in the fever of the sudden giant coups he was raking in, he decided he hadn't noticed the now heavy fall of the dice. If there was a "fix" in, Bello, so far at least, seemed unaware of it.

But it was clear to Joe. Somebody had taken advantage of his byplay—his somewhat less than rapt attention to the board, and had pushed queer dice into action.

He started away from the table. The secretary followed, asking: "What'll I do with this?"

Joe paused only an instant, then pointed out Sunny. "Type it up and give it to her."

Then he went straight to the office.

Sprig looked grim, unshaven. ("Old High Pockets," Joe used to call him: long and lean. "The barefoot boy." Because he liked to take his shoes off when he wasn't in public.) He had his shoes off now, and in his stocking feet had a two hundred pound, six-foot three, moon-faced man backed up against the wall. The big man was sweating. Carlos Ochoa and Bill Rux, two of Sprig's best undercover boys were present. All turned to look at Joe, their eyes asking why he was here.

"We're getting a dice switch," Joe said.

Sprig nodded wearily. "I know. I've been tracking it for eight solid hours. What did they do, put it back in?"

"You mean it was in before?"

"Yeah. Must have happened during the dawn break—while you were resting. I was pretty busy. But the moment Bello came back, he began having fantastic luck. Except that it wasn't luck."

"Shaved dice?"

"That's it," Sprig said, "but they must be the world's

best. I've sent four boxes up to the police lab. I'll get a report any minute."

"What about the feed in? Who in the hell's doing it?"

"Joe, just go back to the table and keep both eyes wide open. I'm close to this now. I'll have the whole thing lifted and out of here in the next half hour. Go back and act like it's all right—nothing's wrong. If you scare them now, it'll take me longer."

"Right." One thing he had learned was to trust Sprig implicitly: ask no questions. Let him run his end of the show.

He returned to the dice table. Bello was still pulling in chips. The sudden bonanza had picked him up physically: he wasn't even concerned that Joe had been gone for a couple of minutes. Joe stood and watched him win on throw after throw of the bad dice. His stomach was churning, he wanted to shut down the table—run everybody and his brother out of the pit. But he did nothing and his face was without expression.

Twenty-two minutes later, the shift of croupiers was replaced—at the normal time for the change-over. But Sid Manners, the pit boss, brought fresh boxes of dice, and picked up the current dice from the table and boxes. He did it unobtrusively—Bello scarcely noticed, and thought nothing of it—but Joe knew that standard, honest dice were now coming back into the game and he said a silent word of thanks to Sprig.

In the office, Sprig now had the culmination of eight hours work: tedious, painstaking, relentless investigation. Besides the beefy, moon-faced man Joe had seen backed to the wall, there were two other strangers. The door opened and Sid Manners came in with the stickman from the crew who had just been relieved from the main table.

Sprig gazed at the four, his bloodshot eyes burning. Ochoa and Rux lined them up. "Like a police line-up,"

Sprig said. His voice was hoarse now, and experts in the trade knew enough to be afraid when he spoke like this. The words seemed to come from the pit of his stomach.

"I have the report from the police lab—and the facts about all four of you. You, the manufacturer of these dice." He threw a handful of the large, red, razor-sharp edged dice fully into his fat moon face. "You even have a legitimate-looking dump of a factory in town. Who set you up—gave you the money to start?"

The man's face was bleeding. "Why, I—I started months ago."

"I *know* it was months ago, chum."

"If there's anything wrong with these dice—it must be my machines. Maybe they're out of line."

"Yeah—they're out of line. Like you're out of line. They were built out of line."

The stickman, white-faced, said: "When they handed me the new dice, I thought they were the regular—"

Sprig crossed and slashed him with his bony fists, then stepped back.

"I ought to kill you—all of you. But if chummy here—" he returned to the manufacturer, "will speak up loud and clear about who backed him in the loaded dice business—"

"I don't know! The contact disappeared after the first few meetings."

"Then you *were* set up?"

"He said the buyers would be around later."

"So who are the buyers?"

The manufacturer was miserable. "This wasn't the only sale I had. People found out I had shaved dice and wanted them."

"People wanted dice loaded *against* the house? I thought it was mostly small joint bandit club owners that were in the market for this kind of an operation. They'd want them working *for* the house—not against it!"

"Yes. But I had orders for *both* kinds."

"So you had a lot of buyers—and what you're trying to tell me is, you don't know who bought this particular batch?"

"No, honestly I don't! It could have been a customer a couple of months ago—or last week."

"And naturally a man who deals in phony dice doesn't keep books?"

"No."

Sprig believed him. He backed up a few steps now. His head was throbbing; his body was racked from exhaustion.

"All right, boys, get out of here—and I never want to run into any of you anywhere, any time, any place in this town, because if I do, you're going to bleed a little from a lot of different places!"

The four men filed out one after the other, almost unable to believe their good luck at going scot free, and Rux said:

"Chief, let me get you some coffee—a sandwich."

"Could use," Sprig said. He sat down behind the desk. He hadn't eaten in two days.

"Shall I tell Joe it's cleaned up?"

"No, he knows by now."

Rux left, and Sprig looked at Ochoa. "Wonder where it'll come from next?"

"You expect more?"

"Yeah," Sprig said, "more."

Half an hour later, in the telephone room in downtown Las Vegas, Wily, a thickset man who wore glasses—and the only human being in town who knew the identity of the group behind Bello—was talking long distance to his bosses. He was reporting on Sprig.

"He's uncanny—I don't know how he does it! Stops us at every turn. Threw the queer chips out right away—and now the loaded dice are gone for good. He has wires everywhere."

"Do something about him," Wily was told.

"What *can* I do?"

"Don't you know?"

Wily was shocked into silence. "But it's too late now. He's done the big damage."

"He can do more."

"I don't know what."

The voice at the other end of the wire grew harsh. "Find *you*, maybe—trace *us!* I gave you an order!"

Wily was sweating now. "But I doubt anyone could get through to Sprig. He has layers of protection—a network."

"Try."

Wily still protested. "I don't know anybody in town who'd do it."

"What town *do* you know somebody in?"

"Chicago."

"Get him."

Wily licked his dry lips, half whispered. "It'll cost five hundred and the round-trip ticket."

"Cheap."

"All right."

He hung up, emerged from the booth and walked up to the busy and harassed operators. After several minutes he got the attention of one of them and placed a person-to-person call to Chicago.

Nineteen

The playing cards used in blackjack games are washed every afternoon by several young women seated at a long table in the counting room. They also check the cards for creases, damage or the telltale marks of a professional cheat. A deck with even one damaged or marked card is thrown away; the rest are wiped clean with a cloth that has been dipped in a special solution. At another table, a few feet away, strongboxes taken from beneath the gaming tables are opened and the money inside carefully counted by men expert at such things, the money being checked against the amount of chips allotted to the table at the start of the session.

It was going on three o'clock when Mal entered the casino. He was just back from Boulder City. Dee would arrive a few minutes later, through a different door. He gazed around, saw that all four of the crap tables were going, a fair crowd patronizing them, several of the men (guests at the hotel) wearing open sports shirts and no coats, and a few clad in swimming trunks, sandals and a tee shirt. Everything seemed quiet, casual. The big game was operating the same as before: a crowd of Vegas people thronged around it.

He felt hungry and started for the adjoining buffet when he saw Sunny Guido headed in the same direction. He caught up with her.

"Could I buy you a lunch—a sandwich—food?"

She smiled. "How about Dutch treat?"

"Are schoolteachers always so proper?"

She laughed. "They try to be." But thinking of Joe, she wasn't laughing, and the word "proper" upset her. How proper had she been early this morning when he pulled off the bed covers?

They found a table in view of the big crap game, ordered a light lunch; he noticed her eyes turning again and again in the direction of Joe.

"You and Joe getting along all right?"

Wondering whether he knew she was now living in the penthouse, she flushed, but answered: "I like him a lot."

"So do I. That makes two of us."

He shot her a quick look and decided Joe must have scored. But he had his own problems. Dee. They had talked more than two hours trying to find a realistic way out. "Old Mal Davis and his advice to lost and confused human beings," he had said. "If you want the truth, I think I need advice more than you do." "Why," she'd asked, "what's wrong with you?" "Forget it. We're not here to talk about me." And they didn't. They had sipped endless cocktails and discussed *her* problem and finally didn't agree on anything except that they'd somehow meet again —and maybe by that time he'd have a plan. But meet *where?* "Certainly not in public," he'd said. "Maybe in some cheap out-of-the-way old hotel downtown. And don't think—don't think for a minute I say a hotel room because I have anything dirty on my mind. I won't so much as try to touch you." She believed him and asked him to arrange for the room, and he'd promised to do so first thing tomorrow. It'd be after 1 A.M., when he was off the piano. How to slip away from Bello again was something *she* was going to have to work out.

Old Mal Davis, he thought now, on his sturdy white charger, wearing his shining white plume. Who am I kidding? I can't even help myself!

The food came and he ate, trying not to think about it any more. Two tables away he noticed a stately young woman who was a customer from the swimming pool area. She was garbed in a yellow bathing suit and matching sandals, with a smart, stiff-collared black half-coolie coat draped over her shoulders. He could see her long, lean, tanned legs under the table. There was something familiar about her. Suddenly he knew…she was Kitty Erin—a TV actress. He'd met her in Palm Springs.

When he and Sunny finished, he insisted on paying

the check after all, then left her there at the table, with apologies. He stopped by Kitty Erin's table and said "Hello," then walked outside.

A minute or two later, Sunny finished her second cup of coffee and was ready to get up when a woman stopped in front of her. "Are you—yes, you must be."

"Must be what?" Sunny wanted to know.

"I'm the public stenographer here. Mr. Martin dictated something a couple of hours ago. It would have been finished before now, but Mr. Sprig had work that couldn't wait. I'm sorry."

"Mr. Martin *dictated* something?"

"Yes. Said it was for you—pointed you out. I've been looking for you. Here it is."

She held out a sheet of paper.

Sunny took it, bewildered, then sat back down and looked at it. It was typewritten.

J. to S.
    Subject: Some of the data you wanted on my past.
    Age 8. Got a paper route. Am only child. Parents not rich, not poor—more poor than rich, though. They are both forty to fifty years old. Older than other kids' parents. Sort of Blah. Best thing about them is they leave me alone—come and go as I like. So I'm alone a lot. Father a jeweler. Small shop somewhere. Doesn't talk much. Reads newspaper all the time. Mother helps him at the jewelry shop.
    Age 9. Now selling papers on a corner instead of delivering them. Step up. More money. Also making money from various pastimes like lagging or matching coins. I always figured a way to get the "edge."
    Age 11. Approached by bookie to take local horse bets from customers for a commission.

Age 12. Began booking the smaller bets myself (without telling bookie) and began then to make big money.

At fourteen I didn't run away from home—I drove away—in a pretty good little car that was all paid for and all mine. Just walked out of the house and kept going. I'll bet it was weeks before my parents looked up one day and discovered I was gone.

Went to New York City and got a job as

It ended there, abruptly, in the middle of a sentence.

When she finished reading, she was startled to see Joe standing there gazing down. "That the thing I dictated?"

"Yes."

"You mean you just now got it?"

She rose slowly. "Joe, why aren't you at the dice table?"

"Bello wants a break. Two hours."

She stared at him. "Any reason?"

"Sprig tells me it's girl trouble. But I think it goes farther. He's folding a little—wants to take a nap to refresh himself."

"Good! That means *you* can get some sleep."

He shook his head. "No, no sleep. We're going to Lake Mead."

"Lake Mead? But you need *rest!*"

"What I need is to talk to you."

She felt her face flush.

"Swim...and talk to you," he was saying. "No, we won't even swim. We'll just get wet, and we'll talk. We'll talk in the water neck deep."

"But if this game is going to go on—"

"Oh, it's going to go on," he said, "on and on. But let's not think of it now."

"But—"

"Quit arguing, Sunny. I don't want to change my mind. I don't want to change the way I feel right now."

"All right, darling. I won't argue."

"Go up and get your bathing suit. I'll meet you at the car."

Joe and Sunny drove off the premises at 3:22 P.M.

Exactly four minutes later, the phone rang in Sprig's office. He picked it up and spoke scarcely a word, just listened, as Rux and Ochoa watched him. At last Sprig said: "Thanks very much," and hung up. Though he was wan, weary, he seemed pleased now, excited.

"That was Chicago—a tip."

(The man Wily had been right. Sprig *did* have wires everywhere.)

"And I have news for you, boys. The syndicate that's trying to bust Joe—they're a little upset. The fact is, they're beginning to panic!"

Rux asked: "What happened?"

"A two-bit Chi torpedo will be here on the midnight plane."

Ochoa groaned. "How can they be that crude?"

Sprig only smiled, rubbing his bony hands together. "They're beginning to act like amateur night in Dixie. Means we've got them on the ropes. And we're going to keep them there."

"Don't they know," said Rux, "that a hood hasn't a chance in Vegas?"

"If they did, they've forgotten," Sprig answered. "Because this is dumb. Real dumb. They're playing right into my hands!"

"Who's he supposed to kill—Joe?"

"*Me,*" Sprig said. He was so happy, he got up and paced the room. "Isn't that beautiful? I've upset some of their flipping plans. So they're mad. They're sulking. They want revenge. Sprig's bright red blood. Well, they'd play hell getting it even if I *hadn't* gotten the call. That gorilla

would have been spotted the moment he walked in."
Sprig kept pacing. "Trouble is, we would have rousted him
out and that's all. Never would have known what was in
his evil little mind. But now it's juicy—good and juicy."

"We meet him at the plane?" Ochoa asked.

"No, we'll just be there—in the woodwork, watching
to *see* who meets him; then we'll follow them, and the
man we want to nail *isn't* the torpedo—it's the one who
pays him and gives him his instructions. Because he'll
know who it is we're dealing with—what group it is." He
sighed. "Oh, I love this! Boys, our work isn't without certain compensations now and then."

"A guy's coming to bump you off, and you love it," Rux
teased.

"Oh, I do, I do—nothing I like better than to see the
expression on their potato faces when you pull the rug
out from under them."

Twenty

Heat was rising in shimmering layers visible to the eye,
and Lake Mead, its shores and water deserted in the
swelter of heat, lay flat and motionless, like a giant blob
of steel, mirroring torrid sunlight. A short drive from Las
Vegas, the casino brochures that advertised it as a gay
resort with swimming, fishing, boating and camping sites
for tourists exaggerated outrageously. It was no more
than a bleak desert lake with a hilly, craggy bank that
sheltered hidden coves and inlets.

Joe had driven fast. The top was down on the car, and
with wind whipping by, neither he nor Sunny had spoken.
She was clad in a bathing suit, wearing a short coat over it,
and beach sandals. He parked the car in a lonely section,

directed her to a spot facing the water, then changed to trunks he had in the back of the Cadillac.

When he joined her, she was seated in the sand, almost broiling under the rays of the sun. But she looked up with a half smile.

"Got a job as what?"

He flopped down beside her, feeling faint for a moment. He *was* exhausted, *did* need sleep; yet he was buoyant, and determined to hold this feeling, this soaring feeling that was lifting him, exciting him. "What? What job?"

"Your note. You left home—went to New York."

"Oh. That. The drab, dead past."

"I want to know."

"Why?"

"You were only fourteen—how could you get a job?"

"Easy. Box boy. And I corrupted the whole company. With a pair of dice. Had games going all the time in the back room. *I* didn't play—just kept watch—and collected a percentage off the top for organizing and running things."

"A casino owner at a tender age."

"No—owner of a floating crap game. They caught up with me, finally—fired me. But the die was cast. I knew how to make a buck without risking a penny. Formula for easy living."

"*Did* you live easy?"

"I've always lived easy. I don't want to talk about the past any more." He was holding his hand up to shield his face from the sun. "There isn't much variation in my past. I've never been able to trust anybody much. Never had any what you'd call real friends. I've lived alone with a million people around me. Just like the way I was raised —alone, with two parents there in the same house. Only I don't eat out of the icebox any more. I can buy anything and anybody I want."

"*Anybody?*"

"I didn't mean it personally. Literally."

"But you've been in love, of course?" She was studying him, his hard, lean face running with sweat now.

"I'm beginning to doubt it."

"But surely—"

"No—don't try to pry and peek any more. My yesterdays are my own—dull, stupid—and all of them too intense; God, I've been going like a freight train all my life."

"And getting places," she said.

"I'm already there—that's why I called it 'Rainbow's End.' "

"And *is* it?"

"I thought so for a while."

"Don't you now?"

He looked at her. "I'm wondering."

She didn't feel the sun now, and she was no longer conscious of the stifling, baked air that was so hard to breathe. "Why, Joe?"

He jumped up. "Let's go in the water."

He held out his hand and she took it and he pulled her up; they walked into the water together. It was crystal clear and almost warm—yet cool enough to be refreshing. They walked out shoulder deep.

"This is better," he said.

"Much better."

"I feel alive again."

"So do I."

He held her at arm's length, inspecting her, then pulled her to him and they kissed deeply. Afterward he said: "Know what I've been thinking?" He paused. "I'm almost afraid to say it out loud."

"*Please* say it out loud."

"That maybe I'd like to quit—quit and get out. Quit the worry, the fuss, the bother; quit the kind of thing that's going on now—a marathon crap game with a casino for the winner. Quit the whole flipping mess."

The word offended her. "Joe—"

"And get a boat," he went on, "a *hell* of a boat; trim, streamlined. As a kid, I always used to think of boats. I had a little collection of them. Dimestore stuff. Do you know it hasn't occurred to me in all this time since I've had a lot of money that I could *buy* one—that I have enough to buy one and live on it and pay a crew and go any goddamn place I want to in the world? Do you know that hadn't occurred to me until I met you—and not even then—not until just the past day or so. And do you know *why?* Don't talk. Just let me tell you why. How can you think of buying a big yacht and living on it alone? Wouldn't that be the most idiotic thing you ever heard of? A man going around the world all by himself—seeing the sights of this whole cockeyed world *alone?*"

She whispered: "I love you."

But he was almost in a trance. "I'd go to the usual ports, of course, all the places everybody else has been except me—Bermuda, Rio, Hawaii—but other places, too. Far places. Arabia. Hong Kong. Istanbul. And Athens. I'd love to see Greece with you, Sunny! I'd like to look at the world with you. You're a schoolteacher, you could teach me about it—and there are things I'll teach you."

"It sounds beautiful, Joe!"

"It sounds insane. But I want to do it. Do you know if Bello breaks me, I won't be able to? But he won't. Hasn't a chance. Will you come with me—on a slow trip all over the oceans that'll last for the rest of our lives?" He peered at her. "Why are you crying?"

"I'm not—it's just—I'm so *happy!*"

His voice was warm. "I'm happy, too. I'm not sure I've ever been happy before—*really* happy."

"I want us to be happy together. To be everything together."

"*Everything?*"

"Yes!"

"You're absolutely sure?"

She was staring at him. "Yes!"

"In every way there is?"

"In every way there is."

"Now?"

"Joe, I—"

He said: "I've just proved you a liar."

"No, you haven't! In every way there is—now!"

"Take off your bathing suit!"

"Here?"

He nodded.

"Won't somebody—"

"Nobody'll see."

She reached around to unzip it, and then he helped her, peeling it off her chest; she was breathing hard, her breasts bobbing in the semi-warm water. He kept pulling at the suit, sliding it off her hips, then made her step out of it. He tossed it ashore. Then, a moment later, his trunks followed. Sunny was quivering now as he approached. She closed her eyes, and felt his hands on her hips. Now, suddenly, she half screamed, her whole body shaking.

His hands still on her hips, he lifted her up and carried her to the beach and lowered her and himself to the sand; and then she was writhing, moaning, eyes still closed, pain shooting through her.

"What's the matter?"

"Nothing, darling."

"Hurt?"

"No, everything's lovely."

He was very gentle now and kissed her mouth, her neck, her ears; and all at once she forgot the pain, it wasn't there; and she clutched at him, pulling him closer to her, and she thought she was going to faint.

"Oh, Joe—"

"I love you," he said. "God help me, Sunny, I love you, I really love you."

"I love you, too!"

"We're fine now, aren't we?"

"Yes, darling—everything's fine—except—I'm running out of breath."

"I want you to run out of breath."

"Am I—am I supposed to talk to you?"

"No," he said, "there are times when you won't be able to. At least I hope there will be."

"I think I'm reaching one of those times."

"We both are."

Twenty-one

7:22 P.M.

Mal was at the piano. He'd been there about ten minutes when a girl in a tight silk dress sat down on one of the stools—a thin wisp of a thing, completely unpretty, with big eyes and garish lipstick. She was hardly settled when a uniformed casino policeman walked up, helped her down again, and then catching her elbow moved away a few feet and spoke firmly. She left without fuss, heading for the nearest exit.

Prostitution in Las Vegas is strictly controlled and she was evidently an "outlaw"—trying to do a little hustling on her own. Most of the big sporting houses are in a nearby small town that can be reached by taxicab for a flat two dollars and a half; and the girls, once you get there, will entertain you for prices that range from ten to fifteen to twenty dollars. There are several houses in Vegas, too, on the outskirts, but not as fancy; and the talent is usually inferior to that found in the bawdy-gaudy salons of the small town. But the highest-class and highest-priced whores are right in the Strip casinos—call girls who will come to your room for fifty dollars and stay the entire night if you double the ante.

The customer beside whom the wispy little "outlaw" had briefly sat down was a Big Man on a small scale. He wore an almost offensive green suit, with a red-checkered flannel hunting shirt, and had money spread out on the piano bar before him in the shape of a fan—hundred dollar bills, fifties, twenties, tens and ones: the idea being, apparently, that he didn't like to fish for his wallet every time the cocktail waitress brought him a drink. But he didn't fool anybody, particularly Mal, who had seen his type before—and was always embarrassed for them.

"My name's Si Shelby," he said, standing and reaching over the piano to shake hands with Mal, who had to stop playing for a moment, get up and let his hand be gripped. "I'm from down L.A. way."

Mal mumbled that he was glad to meet him, sat down, and resumed playing.

Shelby was a big man, with a broad face and bright, sharp eyes. He was a year or two this side of forty, his wavy brown hair thinning on top. If you could stomach his overbearing manner, he was vaguely handsome, and made a great effort to be flamboyant, likable—good fellow to everybody.

"I'm in the used car game."

Mal felt he *had* to speak, and asked: "How is the used car business these days?"

"Making nothing but money," Si Shelby said, "nothing but money—hand over fist."

Mal didn't know why, but he felt the man was a terrific

liar. People who make big money usually play it down or complain about the tax bite.

Shelby shoved a dollar bill toward him. "Play *My Melancholy Baby.*"

Mal pushed the dollar back and a couple on the other side of Shelby, too embarrassed to stay any longer, got up and left.

"No tips," Mal said.

Angry now, nervous and upset by Shelby, he began to play the request. And Dee appeared—the same as last night. It was as if he had blown a whistle for her. She found an empty cocktail table for two near the piano and sat down. Over at the crap table, Bello had his back to them, and seemed deeply engrossed, while Joe scowled at almost every roll of the dice. Mal smiled openly at Dee, and she smiled back, then averted her eyes.

"Five...five a point. Will he or won't he five?" ("Phoebe, dice! One time! Little Phoebe!") *"Six, the point is five."* ("This time, dice!") *"Seven, loser. Line away. A brand-new shooter. Do or don't come. Will he or won't he? Who wants the odds on craps or eleven? Coming out now — Ee-o-leven! Pay the line..."*

Mal had turned back to the keyboard when he saw the house resident physician approaching—Doc Hoffman: husky, tanned, wearing a suit and tie. Mal knew him casually and liked him. He was off duty now, and took a stool at the piano.

"Is there anything special you'd like to hear?"

"No, you name it."

Mal started into a medley and played and sang for several minutes, now and then sneaking a half smile at Dee. Doc Hoffman wasn't just enjoying the music, he was practically living it—and Mal knew he was a real fan. He slacked off, strumming the ivories with light instrumental music.

"Doc, you live in Las Vegas all the time?"

The doctor nodded. "I haven't been anywhere else in six years."

Mal gazed at him curiously. "How can you stand it? It'd drive me crazy if I was here that long."

Doc Hoffman shrugged. "*I* think it's paradise."

"You have to be kidding."

"No. To salve my conscience for having things so good, I spend two hours every morning in the free clinic at the hospital. Directly after that, two hours in a little office I have downtown with a private practice. The rest of the day is my own. The casino pays my room and board, and I'm on hand from about four in the afternoon until midnight. After that, I can be reached wherever I go."

Mal nodded. "Yeah—but the same rat race, day after day; the same dice chant—"

"You get accustomed to it. Besides, I don't gamble, so there's no attraction. They hate me for not gambling, but what are they going to do? I like to swim. I see all the fine shows and date an interesting variety of beautiful women this town is full of. Hell, I live off the fat of the land. How could anybody, anywhere, have it so good?"

Si Shelby interjected: "*I'm* sold. I was going to head for Mexico City—but now I've definitely decided to stay right here." The cocktail waitress arrived, and he told Diane: "Drinks for everybody at the piano. See what they'll have, honey."

Mal and Doc exchanged looks, but didn't protest; whenever a big spender wants to buy for the house it's less wear and tear if you merely accept. And now the tall, very lovely Kitty Erin was sitting down on the stool next to Doc. She nodded at Mal, smiled. Si Shelby stared at her rudely. And when Diane returned with the drinks, said:

"One for her, too."

The TV actress looked over at Shelby, smiling thinly. "Thank you, but no." Her voice was soft.

"But I'm buying a round for the whole piano," Shelby explained.

She shook her head, then quietly gave her order to Diane.

"Eight, the hard way. Eight, eight a point — Six, the point is eight — Eight, easy eight. Eight, the winner...."

Cottontop approached the piano now, looking excited. The little breakfast room waitress, garbed in a sleeveless red summer dress, had appeared out of nowhere. She was clutching an autograph book in her hand. She climbed up on the last empty stool and peered past Shelby and the Doctor toward Kitty Erin. Mal sensed she was going to talk no matter what he was trying to do with music, so he took a brief break, sipping the highball Shelby had bought for him.

"I'm sorry to bother you, Miss," Cottontop said, "but aren't you—don't tell me, it'll come to me in a second! You're on TV a lot. And your name is—would you sign my book, Miss Erin?"

With everyone staring at her, Kitty Erin squirmed uneasily. "All right."

Cottontop climbed off the stool, and came around to her, thrusting the book forward. "Write 'To Cindy'—that makes it more *personal.*" Then, before the actress could write anything, she went on: "Why don't you get in the movies, too? You're wonderful. I mean you're so *young* and everything."

"Thank you. I'll talk to my agent about it."

She at last began scribbling in the autograph book, and at the same time the loud-speaker in the casino began to page: *"Mr. Rock Hudson, you are wanted on the telephone in the lobby. Mr. Rock Hudson..."* Cottontop's head jerked up. For a moment it seemed as if she would yank the book away from Kitty Erin, but she somehow managed to contain herself for another half second. Then, when the book was handed back, she mumbled a fast, "Thank you very much," and darted toward the lobby telephones.

"A real character," Mal said.

"I knew I'd seen you somewhere," Si Shelby said. "TV, huh? My name's Si Shelby, Miss Erin."

She ignored him. "Mal, remember that song I used to request so much in Palm Springs?"

"*Angel Eyes?*"

"That's it. Will you play it?"

"Sure will." He fingered through the intro, then began to sing.

Try to think that love's not around,
Still it's uncomfortably near...

Cottontop returned in a dirge of disappointment and sat down next to Shelby. "He didn't show up. He isn't even in the casino. Can you imagine that—Rock Hudson isn't even in the casino!"

My old heart ain't gaining no ground,
Since my Angel Eyes ain't here...

He finished the song, and was taking another sip of his drink when he heard the remarks of men who were moving past.

"Joe's had it—really had it. I predict he'll lose this place inside of another twenty-four hours."

"Yeah—Bello's in stride tonight, no doubt about it. He's going in for the kill."

It tensed Mal; he gazed over at the main crap table, noticed the furrows on Joe's face.

"Vegas," Doctor Hoffman was saying to Kitty Erin, "fun place of the world."

Twenty-two

Although the house frowns on a stickman using the vernacular of the players: *"Box cars"*—for two sixes; *"Big Dick"* for ten; *"Quinine" (the bitter dose)* for nine; *"Phoebe"* for five; *"Little Joe"* for four; *"Snake eyes"* for two ones—he is permitted to make a litany of his chant: give rhythm, poetry, even a hit to the unending flow of calls. *"Coming out, bets down, Ee-o or any…"* And without changing his frozen expression lace in subtle humor. If one or both dice fly up into the wooden rack, it's "No good in the wood," or hop skip into the glass dice bowl: "No roll in the bowl."

But tonight nothing was funny to Bello. His face was like granite. He had shaved, changed clothes, looked almost refreshed: but deeply angry. And the dice are sometimes slave to an angry and unfrightened player—they were tonight. Joe hadn't seen the last tally, but Bello was close to a million dollars into him.

"I'm doubling all of my bets," the big gambler said suddenly, the words rumbling out. He addressed the box man without looking at Joe. The moneyman started picking up special chips to add to Bello's bets already on the board, but checked with Joe before putting them down.

Joe withheld his decision and now Bello glared at him.

"What's the difference whether I take it from you fast or slow?"

"Policy."

Bello snorted. "A word to hide behind."

The crowd was silent, fascinated. The dice chant stopped an instant, then started up again as Joe scowled at the stickman. But it was the faces around the table that won for Bello.

"Double Mr. Bello's bets," he instructed the box man.

"Six...the point is six, six will win. Eight...the number is six. Place your come and field bets. Four, six is the point. Who wants the hard way?" ("Five—on the hard six! Come on, dice—three and three me!") *"Five—and the number is six..."*

Bello caught Joe's eyes again. "It's only money."

Joe's quick temper flared. "You want it now?"

"And quit the game?" Bello shook his head. "You should be that lucky."

Joe studied him, "What's the needling for?"

"Needling?"

"Something's bothering you."

"Not the dice. *They're* performing beautifully."

"What is it?" Joe demanded.

Bello didn't speak for a moment, but his eyes were locked with Joe's. *"Six, six the winner. Pay the board. Coming out again, the same lucky shooter. Get your bets down...."*

"Policy," Bello said, giving Joe back his word. "I don't like the way you run your business."

Joe was almost livid. "Suppose you explain?"

"You don't know about it?"

"Know about what?"

Both men were keeping their voices low and the conversation strictly personal even though separated by the crap table; an eavesdropper would have to strain to hear. "Ask your top dog security man."

Joe relaxed some now. "He takes care of his business, I take care of mine."

"You tell him to stay out of my life."

"Didn't know he was in it."

People began glancing toward them now, wondering

what was going on, and there was a momentary silence until this outside interest waned.

"Seven—seven out—seven loses. Clear the board. Coming out with a new shooter. Who wants the odds on eleven? Insurance against any craps? Coming out, bets down, do or don't....Four. Four a point. Get the odds on four...."

Bello said: "He tipped me off my girl was meeting somebody this afternoon."

"Did you a favor then."

"One of your employees—is *that* a favor?"

"You insinuating that Sprig arranged it—planted him there?"

"Oh, Mr. Sprig is above that, I suppose?"

"He certainly is."

"*I* don't think so."

Joe was angry again. "Who forced *her* to meet somebody—Sprig?"

"Nobody. She was willing. That's why he was able to damage me. He knew he could damage me. He saw a situation and used it."

"He's a good man, then."

"Yes, he's a good man. But that's dirty pool in the midst of a dice session."

Joe smiled inwardly. "I'll speak to him."

"Tell him to stay away from me. And tell your piano player to stay away from her."

Joe was shocked. "Piano—Mal Davis?"

"Friend of yours?"

"Yes."

"Then tell him it's for his own good."

Joe gazed at the large man steadily. "I see what you mean."

Bello nodded. "Then we understand one another?"

"Yes," Joe said, "thoroughly." Now he lowered his tone

to the point where Bello almost had to read his lips. "But if you ever try anything in my casino—"

"I wouldn't think of it," Bello said aloud.

"Nine—and the point is four. Four will win it. Come bets, field bets. Three—three craps. The number is four..."

"Your casino," Bello said, still needling.

Joe stared at him.

"Ever think of selling out?"

Joe didn't, couldn't answer with the rage that was in his throat. Bello had exercised this particular barb as he went over the million mark into Joe's pocketbook. Bello —the wise and expert gambler. People around the table had tried following his bets but couldn't—they were too complicated. Sometimes he was with and against the house simultaneously. Tonight he was against it—in a crap shooter's paradise because the table was "hot."

At the piano, overlooking all this, Mal was playing an instrumental when Sunny arrived; she took the end stool. Her face was radiant. And he couldn't remember when he'd ever seen her look quite so beautiful.

"Hi," he said.

"Hi, Mal."

Doc Hoffman had left. And now Kitty Erin said "See you later" and moved away. She had grown tired of listening to Si Shelby, who had now latched on to Cottontop, plying her with more drinks than she was used to—for she had protested the last three, then when they arrived, drunk them anyway. Shelby's pitch nauseated Mal: he was a talent scout from Hollywood and she was a very unusual type. Cindy Cottontop, the almost-albino, was in a daze, scarcely able to believe that she, of all people, was an unusual type. When Mal couldn't stand any more of it, he said:

"Did Si tell you he's in the used car business?"

But Cottontop didn't really hear; and if she had, she

wouldn't have believed him—because she wanted to believe Si: wanted to believe him with all her might.

"*Seven, loser. Coming out again now. New shooter. Do or don't come. Take the odds on craps and eleven. Five. Five a number. The shooter can arrive with a five…*"

Mal thought: Life, and the dice keep on rolling.

He heard Cottontop ask: "What's Audrey Hepburn *really* like?"

"Honey, she's one of the sweetest kids you'll ever meet."

The casino was buzzing with a growing excitement—and the noise, all the different and all the combined noises had reached a pitch: a steady, pulsating roar; and the fever, the wildness, the surging giddiness of it was catching. Dee and Sunny were probably his only real piano audience. Dee, who had heard this same roar night after night for endless nights and had immunized herself against it. Mal fell into a crazy sweep of instrumental notes, improvising, adlibbing—background music for a gambling pit: concerto for a casino. The keys were hammering heavy thunder when he faintly heard the voice through the loudspeaker system. He quieted the piano to a whisper and strained to hear the repeat of the message:

"Mal Davis…you are wanted at the telephone. New York City calling…"

He excused himself and a minute or two later was in one of the telephone booths in the lobby.

"Mal!" It was Harry Muller. "Did I interrupt a hot dice game?"

In the short time it took to walk to the telephone, Mal had attuned himself to the call—to the really big news it could bring: that taped session at the La Cienega spot in L.A. with enough tunes in it for a big, fat LP album.

"No—Harry, what is it? Do you have news?"

"Well, it's good *and* bad, Mal. Depends on the way *you*

look at it. Couple of the big companies like you. You, period. The songs are all right—but what they like is the voice. As for the tape we made, they feel it is imperfect."

"The background noise?" He felt himself sinking. "The applause and dishes and all that?"

"No; that didn't bother them. They thought it was sort of unique. But the tape itself is a little scratchy, and the way it was put together just isn't mellow. They won't touch it."

Mal was in a rage. "Why'd you bother to phone? Why didn't you just write me all this crap?"

"If you'll just listen," Harry pleaded. "I'll come to the good part."

"There isn't any good part."

"The top record company in the business wants you to make an album for them."

Mal perked up his ears. "Go on."

"They want you to come back here, backstop yourself with a quintet, and feature voice only. They don't care whether you play piano or not; and they want you to sing standards—something familiar. Like an album of Rodgers and Hammerstein. If that catches on, a few months later they'll let you record an album of your own songs."

"That's flipping nice of them," Mal said, and he was ready to kick the phone booth down. "Did you mention to them that a *piano player* is what I am—and a *composer*— that as far as I'm concerned, the singing is just incidental?"

"Yeah—but they say you're on the wrong kick."

"Flip them. I've lived this long without them. Is this the end of the conversation?"

"No—wait. Christ, Mal—will you quit racing your motor? Let's get back to the La Cienega tape. I've got it sold—provided you go for the deal."

"Thought you said they didn't like it."

"The big companies didn't. But the 'Q' label will take

it…and they're ready to shell out a fifteen hundred dollar advance tomorrow."

Mal fell silent in gloom, discouragement. The "Q" label was one of the cheapest record companies in the business. Their 78 rpm's featured phony names like Lanky Raine, to give the impression it was Frankie Laine, Lori Jay for Doris Day, and blasted with cheap radio advertising that offered three Hit Parade tunes for a dollar. Their more legitimate division sometimes issued 33 rpm Long Playing albums, using the real names of the artists—but always artists who were not yet recognized. They charged a straight six dollars for such a record, but their promotion was poor, and if lightning didn't strike making it catch on, you'd find it a year or so later in cut-rate drugstores selling for $2.95.

"Flip the 'Q' label."

"Is that a final decision?"

Mal felt almost too discouraged to go on talking. "Give me a week. Let me think it over."

"All right, kiddo. You can reach me at the Waldorf."

He hung up, stepped out of the booth and saw both Sprig and Joe waiting for him. They signaled him to a corner of the quiet lobby, but he knew from the way they looked what they wanted: and this was the crusher. One slap followed by another.

"I know, I know," he said. "I'd better stay away from Bello's girl."

"Appreciate it that you played ball, though," Joe told him.

Sprig asked: "But why'd you stay in Boulder City so damned long?"

Mal looked at both of them. "I like her."

"You might like certain poisons if you tasted them, but—"

Mal blew up. "God damn it, he can't keep her a prisoner!"

Joe snapped: "That isn't your worry."

"It ought to be somebody's!"

Sprig realized that he had a task on his hands. "Joe," he said, "you'd better get back to the crap table."

Joe nodded. "Explain the facts of life to him."

When he was gone, Sprig laid it on the line: "You see her any more—and that's it, brother. Bello's given his warning. From here on out, there's no way that I can protect you."

"Whole different conversation from the way it was this morning."

"Yes—that was an errand I wanted done for Joe. Meet a babe in a cocktail lounge. But now I'm telling you not to risk life and limb."

"Thought you said he didn't kill people?"

"Maybe I was conning you."

"No. You're conning me now."

"Mal, believe me, it could be bad—*whatever* he'd do!"

Mal sighed. "Okay, I'll watch myself."

He returned to the piano wondering: what about tomorrow? That cheap hotel room I'm supposed to rent. Can I risk it? Do I *dare* risk it?

Twenty-three

Unless you have a credit card, you cannot cash a check in a Las Vegas casino. If you apply on a weekday they will phone the bank in whatever city you have your account. On a weekend, your chances are slight if not impossible. Yet the intake of checks is astronomical, and they are rushed out each morning on special planes—to the banks in out-of-state cities. If after getting home you remember that gambling in your state is illegal (and that gambling debts are uncollectable by law) and decide to put a "stop" on all those checks you signed in Nevada, chances are you'll find they've already been cashed. If not, and you put a stop on them, you will first get a letter demanding payment—after that, two visitors, very gentlemanly, asking for same—with a hint that the next visit won't be so pleasant. At this point, or shortly thereafter, almost all of the would-be welshers pay up.

"Coming out. Betting time. Do or don't come. Will he or won't he? Is he or isn't he? Get your odds on craps and eleven. Seven! Seven, the winner. Pay that lucky line. Here we go again—get your bets down. Four, four a number. Take the odds on four. Eight, hard way eight. Your number is four, shooter!"

It was now 11:51 P.M. Air conditioning was sucking up the layers of cigarette smoke, yet it seemed to Joe the room was in a blue haze. For hours his stomach had felt hollow, and now it was beginning to suffer the pangs of starvation.

He wiped his hand down over his face to try and snap himself out of it, but couldn't, and then thought: the hell with it!

The tally was now under a million. Bello had lost steadily for the past hour. Joe sent for a waiter and ordered food to be taken to the penthouse, then stayed at the dice table for another ten minutes. When he at last turned to leave, Bello regarded him with surprise. Walk away at midnight—when the pit was at fever pitch?

Sunny was still at the piano, listening to Mal sing, as she had been for hours. When Joe tapped her on the shoulder, she swung around.

"Isn't it time we had something to eat?"

She frowned, glanced toward the dice table. *"Now?"*

He said: "I'll be upstairs," and kept going.

Escorting her through the casino would have caused

gossip; this way, they had simply been observed ex-
changing a couple of words.

Sunny turned back to gather up her purse—and saw
from Mal's eyes that he had guessed the truth of the rela-
tionship. She flushed, and the knowing look left his face;
he pretended to be carried away in a medley.

"See you later," she said.

"Sure thing, teacher."

When she walked away, he watched in awe. He hadn't
heard a word either she or Joe said, but he had seen their
eyes when they looked at each other for that brief moment
—and he *knew*. He thought about it a moment, and was
even more amazed. He'd never seen Joe that way for a
woman. And deserting a big-time game in the heat of it?
But that same look was also in Sunny's eyes. Jesus, what
do you know? Mal thought. The day of the big miracle is
at hand. *Joe?* Joe in love? I would have sworn it wasn't
possible! Well, that just shows you. It's possible for any of
us, dad.

And now his glance shifted to the number one crap
table. Dee was just arriving; she climbed up on the stool
the casino had provided for Bello; and Mal was suddenly
sick inside. He stopped the piano music, sipped a drink;
then decided to take a ten-minute break. He couldn't
stay here and go on watching her with Bello, waiting on
him, lighting his cigarettes—smiling when she was supposed to: pretending interest in an intricate parlay of side
bets that she didn't understand.

In the penthouse, the waiter worked deftly, silently;
he served salad from a bowl nested in ice, added butter
to the steaming baked potatoes, and as a final gesture,
whipped the silvered covers from two browned, juicy
steaks.

After he left, closing the door almost soundlessly, Sunny
kept looking at the snowy clothed table with its inviting

dishes and felt no appetite. When Joe pulled out a chair for her, she sat down automatically.

"Anything wrong?"

His face was wan, cheeks drawn in; even with the crew haircut he seemed not only older, but *old*. Yet he was in excellent spirits and attacked the steak with gusto.

"Are you winning?" she asked. "Is that it?"

"Seesaws."

"Joe, I know you're *tired*—and hungry, but—"

"Why'd I walk out at a peak hour?"

"Yes, why?"

He didn't answer for a moment, then nodded at her dinner plate. "You're not eating."

"I'm not hungry. Anyway, time with you is too precious to spend on eating. I can eat any time. You can't. So go ahead. Finish that salad, and the potato."

"I walked out," he said, obediently following her order, "because I suddenly thought to hell with it—I'm going to act like a human being—crap game or no game. I'm going to eat, nap a little, and look at beautiful Sunny Guido and talk to her." He paused, took a sip of coffee. "I *like* looking at Sunny Guido and talking to her."

She teased. "Why?"

"I'm in love with her." He laughed now. "Imagine *me* carrying on like this!"

"Imagine *me* being here."

"We're going to be everywhere, Sunny. Everywhere worth being is where we'll be. Everywhere except Las Vegas, Nevada. In a teahouse in Tokyo sitting on the floor cross-legged making faces at each other. God, I'm walking on egg shells ten miles up in the stratosphere!"

"I'm up there, too, darling, but—"

"But what?"

"Hadn't you better get back to the dice?"

He scowled. "Why?"

"Joe, if anything happens—you'd blame *me*. You'd say I—*I* kept you from the game."

He relaxed now and looked sleepy. He climbed to his feet, stretched. "You *are* keeping me from the game."

She got up, facing him. "Then *please* go back!"

"After I take a nap."

"Can't you sleep later?"

"Why you little slave driver!" He was angry suddenly, his gray eyes smoky, a cold hardness tightening his lips. "I'm not going to kill myself for him or for anybody else from now on. I'll take care of my business, you take care of yours."

"Mine?"

"Yes. Your business is taking care of me."

"That's what I'm trying to do!"

The edge in her voice infuriated him. He grabbed her violently, started to shake her, then saw the terror in her eyes and didn't. He let go of her and stepped back. "Let's get one thing straight. I don't like being told what to do."

Eyes wide, she said: "You were going to hurt me, weren't you?"

"Did I do it?"

"No, but—"

"Look, Sunny, I'm tired, nervous—hardly know what the hell I'm doing."

"With a temper like that you'll kill somebody some day."

"I never have yet." He had taken off his jacket, was unbuttoning his shirt.

"You said that once before."

"What are we—on *this* again?"

"No, but—that quick, awful temper of yours—it scares me!"

He walked over, stood looking down at her uplifted face. "Then I'll have to learn to curb it," he said simply.

"*Will* you?"

"I'll try. Can't have a little thing like temper fouling up paradise, can we?"

"No."

"This is a beautiful dress you're wearing. Let's not spoil *it*, either." He ran his fingers along the nape of her neck, and then up into her hair, his mouth pressed against her ear as he breathed.

"Joe—" She tried to push away, but felt weak now. Pulling her close against him, he found the zipper on the dress and opened it, kissing her bare shoulder. Exploring down her back, he found the snaps that fastened her brassiere—and suddenly she knew she couldn't resist him and was as wanton as he was, kissing him, clinging to him—her vague fears forgotten: the premonition of danger that might come if he didn't return to the gambling room below.

"I'll take the dress off," she whispered.

"The slip, too."

"Yes, the slip, too."

Moments later, the bed sheet was cool against her back.

Twenty-four

The two most difficult "points" to make are ten and four, since if you rolled anything above or below on the initial "throw," it would be eleven—*natural*, or one of the three *"crap"* numbers: 12, 3, 2. The house will give you two to one odds you won't make a four or a ten. If you want to bet that you will not only make your point, but make it the hard way with two twos (or two fives) they will lay you eight to one against it. If your point is five or nine, you can get a three to two bet against either number showing.

There are no odds on eight or six—it is an even money bet.

It was now 1:03 A.M., and Sprig was unaware of Joe's temporary absence from the big game. He and Rux had been at the airport, waiting for the midnight plane. They had a description of the incoming Chicago assassin but could have spotted him without it the moment he came down the metal ladder. He was thickset, a man in his late thirties; flashily dressed in cheap clothes, he was chewing the stub of a cigar.

When he came through into the terminal, they watched from a distance, made no approach; they were waiting for the real quarry—the man who was going to pay him, the person who knew the identity of the group that was trying to muscle its way into Rainbow's End. All the Chicago torpedo knew or would ever know was that he was to take a fast shot at a difficult target.

But no one met him at the airport. He climbed into a taxi that headed downtown. Sprig and Rux followed. Halfway to Fremont, the cab made a left turn, pulled in at a run-down motel. The flashily dressed hoodlum climbed out, paid the driver and vanished into shadows.

Sprig had already parked his car on the other side of the street, and he and Rux were dashing across the heavily trafficked boulevard to the motel. In the driveway of the place, there wasn't a sound and Sprig was afraid they'd lost him. They walked gingerly past one bungalow after another—nothing.

Then Sprig signaled Rux to stay right here, and cut in between two of the buildings to the side street. He was in time to see the torpedo hurrying across toward a pay telephone in a gas station.

Sprig moved back into the darkness surrounding the motel. He waited until the mobster stepped into the booth, then hurried back and got Rux. The two of them stayed close to the motel, then, watching as the hood stepped out of the booth, looking both ways, and finally lit a fresh stogie.

"Games," Sprig said. But he had new respect for the man who had masterminded them. This, the shaved dice caper and the pushing of queer chips. "Get the car. Be ready to pick me up."

Rux nodded, left, and almost immediately a cab arrived across the street. The hood climbed into it. Sprig watched it drive off, desperately afraid Rux wouldn't get back on time. The seconds seemed endless. Then Rux raced the car up, slowed almost to a stop as Sprig climbed in, and stepped down hard on the accelerator.

It hadn't been much of a chase after that. The cab drove three or four miles—over the railroad tracks, down Bonanza Road, and stopped at an even shabbier motel than the first. Sprig and Rux, unseen and unnoticed, were nevertheless almost on the man's heels as he walked past a single row of cabins and entered number five. They waited then, saw a match light inside, as the hood got his bearings. Then the match went out and the cabin was in total darkness. There was no sound of voices.

That meant the other man would arrive later: would walk around the motel first, casing it to make sure there were no eavesdroppers. Sprig looked for a hiding place where he and Rux could lay low—there wasn't any, none suitable enough to afford them both a view and the ability to hear a conversation from number five.

The other man would get here any minute and Sprig thrashed around for an idea. He glanced at cabin four— dark, probably empty. Yet it was now almost one in the morning and if there *was* an occupant, he might be asleep. However, it was the only move they could make. Enter either cabin four, or six on the other side. Four or six?

Sprig chose four, and with Rux following, opened the door with a pass key. They went in silently, gently pulled

the door shut behind them—still without making a sound.
They didn't dare turn on a light, or even strike a match;
but Sprig gazed around, his eyes growing accustomed to
the dark. He was startled to see a man and a woman lying
asleep on the bed.

He started to open the door, intending to sneak down
to number six when he heard the approach of footsteps.
He pushed the door shut again and he and Rux stood
frozen as the steps grew closer. Presently they stopped.
The man was evidently looking around—doing a pretty
thorough job. At last he moved forward again, and now,
at three minutes past one in the morning, they heard him
enter number five.

There was a sound from the bed in here, and Sprig
glanced at the sleepers. The woman was restless; she
turned on her side. Sprig and Rux were glued to the far
wall where it would be hard to see them. They saw the
lights go on in number five, heard voices.

Sprig opened the door of four, crept out. Rux was right
behind, and Sprig stationed him by the window of five.
He himself inched toward the screen door, careful not to
make a shadow. Now the voices were quite clear.

"…going to be tough."

"I can handle it."

"Ever been in a Vegas casino?"

"No—Florida. Plenty in Florida."

"It's rougher here."

The man who was hiring the hood didn't seem to
believe he could carry out the assignment; yet he was still
determined to have him make the attempt. Means only
one thing, Sprig thought, he's acting on orders: which I
knew all the time. But this confirms it. He's the boy
I want, so why wait any longer?

He drew a gun from his waist, yanked open the screen
door and barreled in.

"Don't make any—"

But the man Wily, terror-stricken, was between Sprig and the hood. He made a wild leap for the window, his shoulders crashing through the rotted screen.

Rux saw a flash of him coming out, thought he had a gun and opened fire.

Sprig pistol-whipped the hood all the way to the floor, then relieved him of his gun and stepped out to see what had happened. The couple from number four, sheet-draped, were gaping out the window. Other people were coming on the run.

"It's all right," Rux told them, "police."

Sprig was examining Wily, and now he groaned. "I wanted him alive!"

"He isn't?"

"Not so you can notice it." Before he got up, Sprig deftly felt to see whether Wily had a gun and only now noticed that he had died and fallen from the window ledge with one hand in his pocket. Quickly, before the gathering spectators could notice, Sprig pulled the dead hand out. It was clutching a gun, the fingers still gripping it tightly.

Sprig put the hand holding the gun gently on the ground, then told Rux: "Get Sampson."

Sampson was in the sheriff's office.

Paying no attention to the crowd, Sprig returned to the cabin where the hood was climbing to his feet, wiping blood from his face, and noticing with dismay that some of it had splattered his suit. He looked up now, glaring, and Sprig gave him the back of his hand, hard, sending him reeling back.

"You cheap little punk, we don't even let punks like you play at the tables in Rainbow End!"

"Who are—"

"Sprig. John Sprig."

The hoodlum gaped.

"*You* got a name, punk?"

"Todman."

"I'll tell you what, Todman, you're going back to Chicago and spread the news of the kind of reception we give to visiting punks."

Todman was shaking now. "What—what are you going to do?"

"Take you for a nice ride out into the desert. A hundred miles or so in the direction of Utah. Ought to be just about daylight when you get there. From that point you can walk the two hundred miles or so to the next town. Barefooted. On a highway so hot it'll blister your feet— and with nothing but desert on either side of you."

Todman started to say: "You can't—"

"*What?*" Sprig cut in, his face tight.

Todman subsided.

"Maybe if you're lucky," Sprig told him, "you'll be able to hitch a ride. I guess you're going to have to. You won't have any shoes—or any money."

Todman sat down, nursing his battered face.

The sheriff's car drove in a few minutes later, and Sprig went out and met it.

The Third Day

Twenty-five

In the days of the old West, the most popular gambling game was faro—which was played by taking cards from a box. But in 1880, John Winn, a professional dice maker, designed and built the first crap table: thus getting the dice players up off their knees and giving dignity to the game. It was Winn who developed the system of how to "bank" the play with a slight percentage favoring the house. That was the beginning of the end of faro—which was dead by the start of the twentieth century.

It was nearly 5 A.M. and Mal had been on the same bar stool for hours watching Dee at the table beside Bello. She seemed tied to the big gambler, devoted, attentive, and for a few wild minutes he wondered whether she had been giving him a snow job that afternoon—conning him: something to amuse herself. Maybe she'd pulled the same thing on any number of men. If so, what kind of a female trap was he walking into?

But he thought it over and decided he was wrong. He'd seen her tears and they had been real tears. He'd heard her voice, looked into her eyes. So why not go on with this project? Please, God, let me do something good once in my life, something decent! I'll *get* that hotel room tomorrow. I *will* work out a solution for her.

He was deep in this reverie when someone slapped him on the back—too hard, and he turned and saw Si Shelby. The used car dealer was still wearing the open hunting shirt, and the same sickly green suit.

"Hi, Krazycat!"

When Mal didn't answer, he flopped down on the

nearest bar stool, snapped his fingers for the bartender; the man didn't immediately respond, and he gave a short shrill whistle to attract him. By this time Mal was ready to crawl under the stool.

"Double Scotch over rocks, and see what Krazycat here'll have," Shelby said when the bartender came over. "You hear the latest, Krazycat? Bello's a million and a half into the casino owner here."

A real bloodletting, Mal thought.

"And you know something?" Shelby continued. "The guy's fantastic. I've been hearing about him for years. When he's on a streak like this, a man could make a fortune just following his bets."

Mal shook his head. "His bets are too complex and mathematical to follow; anybody that'd attempt it would go crazy trying to decipher what he's doing."

"I wouldn't say that, Krazycat. I'm pretty good at figures."

Mal looked over coldly. "Where is this car lot you own?"

"Down in L.A."

"But *where?* On Vermont; or is it Beverly Hills, Hollywood, or the Valley? Maybe I've passed it."

Si Shelby seemed suddenly nervous. "Valley," he said, mumbling the word.

Mal, conscious that he was rattling him, began to press. What he hoped to prove was that he either wasn't a used car dealer at all, or owned only a small operation. "Oh. North Hollywood? Van Nuys?"

Shelby tensed. "Why? What's the difference? You live in the Valley?"

Mal pretended to be hurt. "Yeah. And I just thought I might know where the lot is."

"North Hollywood."

"Under your name?"

"Yeah. Shelby Car Company. Only I closed it down. Sold out."

"But you said you were making money hand over fist."

"I *did;* so I'm retiring for a couple years. A man can't work all the time."

"No, that's right."

"Jesus, Krazycat, you act like a prosecuting attorney."

Mal's suspicion began to solidify. Men with nothing to conceal are glad to identify their place of business: in fact, they bore the hell out of you with every last detail. He'd had to drag the information from Shelby—who was still squirming, restless, and sweating a little. Mal released him from the tension by changing the subject.

"How'd you make out with Cottontop?"

"Who?"

"Cindy—the girl with the white hair and the autograph book."

"Oh." Shelby took a sip of his drink, and began to compose himself; he felt a lot better.

"You were telling her you were a talent scout."

"Yeah—and that old moth-eaten line still works."

"Really?"

"Nothing to it. Slam-bam—thank you, ma'am."

Mal wanted to hit him, knock him right off the stool; but he betrayed no emotion. "That easy, eh?"

"Well, she was drunk, you know. I mean *drunk.*"

"That couldn't be because you kept urging her to drink up so fast?"

"Could be."

"Seems to me you taught her how to play chug-a-lug."

"And she was dumb enough to think gulping them down like that was really a game."

"Well, it *was* sort of a game," Mal said.

"It sure was. Only she was so stupid drunk, she got on a crying jag."

"Oh, did she cry?"

"Moment I started messing with her."

"Didn't resist, though?"

"No, she was limp, dead weight, and sobbing the whole time."

"Why would she cry?"

"Who knows why drunks cry."

"Maybe God does," Mal whispered.

"Who?"

"Never mind."

He was thinking of Cottontop with her twenty-five year old body and her thirteen-year old mind. What would *Movie Idol Magazine* have to say about this?

Shelby slugged down his drink, snapped his fingers for the bartender and ordered two more. Then he returned to his original thought: "I'm telling you, with a hot lick like Bello's got, a man could make a fortune following his bets!"

He turned on the stool and looked at the table where Bello was playing. "I'm tempted." Mal turned around, too.

"You understand dice, the odds and all that?"

"Anybody can play dice," said Shelby. "I've played dice for years. Look, he's still winning."

"How can you tell?"

"The casino owner is having a quiet fit." The drinks were put on the table behind them, and Mal reached back and got his, but Shelby showed no interest. "I'm losing money just sitting here. Want to know something—I'm going to take a flyer. I can make myself five or six G's in no time." He climbed from the stool and headed straight for the crowded dice table. Two or three minutes later he managed to edge in close to Bello.

Mal turned back to the bar and looked at Shelby's untouched drink. He managed to finish his own, then was ready to quit. It was five-thirty now and he was not drunk but dead-tired. It had been a long day. He paid for the drinks Shelby had ordered with such a flourish, then moved to the rear door and went out.

Twenty-six

The poor are not wanted in Las Vegas—nor anywhere else in Nevada. Officials sometimes try to get rid of them with an order to move on; however, if a destitute person refuses to budge, the average relief check is fifteen dollars a month. An out-of-funds non-resident of the state has no such choice. He is usually warned if he doesn't depart by a certain hour, he'll go to jail. There is some charity, though: if the impoverished one pleads he has no money for transportation (or no gasoline for his car) and protests that he and his family cannot walk (or push the car) across the scalding desert, he is given enough cash for bus fare, or gasoline, to get him over the county line.

"Eight. Eight, easy. The point is eight. Who wants the hard way? Place your come and field bets. Nine, the point is eight." ("Eighter from Decatur!"—it was Shelby's voice, frantic and shrill, commanding the dice instead of coaxing them.) *"Three, in the field. The number is eight."* ("Eight, dice—make eight, the big eight!")— *"Seven, loser. Seven away. Betting time. Coming out with a new shooter...."*

It was after 7 A.M. now, and the dice were icy cold. Bello had lost back almost a quarter of a million of his winnings, and looked haggard: yet resolute. He was still well over a million dollars ahead and could afford the temporary setback. But one of the other players at the table—a man wearing a green suit and an open hunting shirt looked desperate, wild-eyed. Joe had watched as he clumsily tried to follow Bello's bets—and the more he lost, the more he plunged. By now, three or four thousand dollars had gone down the drain.

A few moments later, Joe looked up and saw Sprig entering the casino. Sprig, tall, skinny, was unshaven, his face mottled. He looked as if he had been dragged up out of a well. Joe left the table and arrived in the office just ahead of him. Ochoa was already inside.

"Where you been?"

"Little errand," Sprig said. He flopped down on the divan.

"All this time?"

"Yes, all this time, Joe."

Ochoa explained: "Somebody came here to kill him."

"That wasn't important," Sprig said, "the important thing was to nail the man who had sent for him."

"*Did* you nail him?"

"No. Killed him."

Joe looked alarmed.

"Don't worry about it," Sprig soothed. "Rux did it— and he's cleared. That's where I've been—sheriff's office." He sat up, rubbing his fists against his temples. "The torpedo is walking barefoot in the direction of Utah by now. Rux drove him out a ways." He gazed up at Joe, his eyes bloodshot. "Any questions?"

"No," Joe said. "If their key man is dead—that ought to be the end of the byplay."

"Ought to be," Sprig responded, "but I don't think it is."

"You don't?"

"No; there's something else going on. I just can't put my finger on it."

"Sprig, you're tired."

"Sure I'm tired."

"Get some sleep."

"Not until I figure out what it is."

"Maybe it isn't anything," Joe argued. "What else could there be? You're so knocked out you're jumping from your own shadow."

Sprig got up stiffly, walked over to the desk, sat on the edge of it. "Don't, Joe. Never interfere with my suspicious mind." He indicated the door. "What's the tally out there?"

"He's about a million and a quarter into us. It was worse, though."

Sprig whistled. "You been sticking right with him?"

"Midnight recess, that's all. Had something to eat, little nap."

"You had a little nap?" His voice was raw.

"What about it?"

"Was the chick up there?"

"Make any difference to you?"

Sprig was off the desk now, facing him, legs spread, jaw jutting. "Yes—it does! *Was* she?"

"Sunny Guido was there—yes. Why?"

"Let me *tell* you why. We're trying to keep the store running. We're out gunning somebody for you. We've got our necks out to here. And what are *you* doing? Watching the table? No—you're letting him zoom ahead of you. That *is* when he zoomed ahead, isn't it? While you were upstairs in your penthouse humping a Wop broad from 'Frisco!"

Joe started to swing, and Sprig shook his head.

"Don't do it. You need somebody around with guts enough to tell you when you're off base. Bello could have walked away with the silverware while you were napping —and he almost did!"

"Look," Joe said, his voice low, shaking, "I'll attend to *my* business—"

"Your business—*our* business—everybody who is part of Rainbow's End—is that crap table out there. Nothing else. Anything or *anybody* that keeps you away from that game while Bello's there—" he suddenly broke off, staring at Joe.

"I think I have it!"

"Have what?"

"What do you really know about Sunny Guido?"

Joe went white. "Enough. I know enough. She's all right. You do have a suspicious mind, don't you? Dirty, low-down and suspicious! Forget it!"

"When she's pulling the floor out from under you?"

"She's not—"

"Holy Toledo," Sprig cut in, "Joe, listen! From the very beginning—the way she hung around here, around *you*—weeks before any of this began! Don't think the group didn't make plans far in advance, because they did. And this tomato—"

"I said lay off!" Joe's fists were still knotted.

"—You wouldn't go for just *any* doll—glamour girl, anything like that. Your hide's too thick. But a school-teacher—a pure, innocent little—"

Joe grabbed him. "Knock it off! And *right now.* You're so tired, you're *sick!* Quit being so overzealous! Your mind rambles on and on—building up a big thing. Well, you're wrong, I'm telling you, you're wrong. You get some sleep and when you have a clear mind again you'll know damn well how wrong you are. And then maybe you'll apologize. But meantime, stay away from Sunny. I don't want you to even *think* about her. That's an order!"

He turned and stormed out of the office.

Sprig was silent for a moment, Ochoa watching him, then he said:

"He's hooked—all the way hooked. I never would have believed it."

"Me, either," Ochoa said. "But Miss Guido seems like—"

"—like an angel," Sprig interrupted. "Sure she does. Hop the first plane to San Francisco and get me a complete rundown on her. Board of Education—her family—and be back by tonight!"

Ochoa was on his feet. "After what Joe said?"

"When he can no longer take care of himself," Sprig said, "it's up to us to do it." He looked at Ochoa. "Go on, get going."

Twenty-seven

Nevada is a marriage mill; over twenty thousand people a year take the vows in Las Vegas alone—probably because it's so quick and easy: drunk or sober, sick or well, you can fly in, get joined in matrimony, and be on your way again in less than an hour. A divorce takes longer—that is, if you're from out of the state. You must establish a Nevada address and live there for six consecutive weeks after which time you are eligible to become a resident. They'll cleave the bonds for you then, though, with dispatch: neatly and bloodlessly; the Las Vegas court, vying with Reno's, cranks out over thirty-five hundred divorces annually.

Mal woke at one-thirty in the afternoon with something prodding him, urging him to hit the floor; still too sleepy to remember what it was, he phoned room service and ordered breakfast, then got up and headed for the shower. The food would be delivered by the time he was shaved, and he could gulp it down, throw his clothes on, and run. Run where? Oh, yeah. The cheap hotel downtown.

Shortly after two o'clock, wearing slacks and a sports shirt, he felt fresh, chipper, and was ready to leave the bungalow. But the moment he was outside the heat closed in, enveloping him, clinging to him soggily, until he was half gasping, his body oozing with sweat. He made his way through the inferno toward the parking lot. The swimming pool was entirely deserted, the water shimmering whitely in the angry glare that burned down from the sky; the glassy tile around it was sizzling in reflected sunlight. This was the peak of the day. The heat might ease off later. There was no guarantee, yet it might; it often did.

But in his car, with the top up, and driving at forty miles an hour, it seemed to get hotter by the minute. He didn't head for Fremont with its downtown gambling emporiums; he parked instead on a business street a few blocks away. It was cluttered with small factories, appliance, hardware and tool stores; and squeezed between them on either side of the street, two shoddy-looking hotels.

He climbed from the car and was now so drenched with sweat, he could have sworn he was melting. He walked over to the entrance of Hotel Cornwall, which was on this side of the street and went inside quickly, expecting relief from the heat. There was none. It was hotter, stickier in the hotel's small lobby than it was outside. No air conditioning. The guests just sweated it out. He turned and made a fast exit. Then he crossed the street to The Mammoth.

It was a commercial hotel, the lobby fairly large; but there were no air coolers here, either—only a large electric fan, droning loudly as it swung back and forth, churning up the humid air. The room clerk, a man in his fifties garbed in dungaree trousers and a tee shirt, was adding a column of figures and though aware of Mal's presence, didn't immediately look up. Mal stood there restlessly, his clothes wet and sticking to him, his face bathed in glistening pools. Finally he said:

"Hey, don't any of these fleabag hotels downtown have air conditioning?"

The clerk, irritated both by the interruption and the insult, carefully made a mark beside the row of figures, then met Mal's eyes.

"Any *what* kind of hotels?"

Mal grinned. "I was needling you, Dad."

"How long do you intend to stay?"

"Just tonight."

The clerk pushed a registration card over, and Mal signed it: *"Mr. and Mrs. Ed Raymond."*

"Oh, your wife is with you?" The clerk glanced around the empty lobby.

"No, she's down on Fremont buying a dress."

"That'll be two dollars."

Mal paid it, and the clerk handed him a key, then returned to his column of figures. Mal looked at the leather tab attached to the key. It was stamped with the name of the hotel and the numerals 203.

It was a small room, facing the street. The two windows were closed, the panes of glass in them dusty and weather-streaked. There was a large bed with a mattress that was lumpy in some places and sagged in others; the brass posters that held it up had evidently once been shiny but the chrome had long ago worn off and the metal was ugly and darkish. The highboy wooden dresser was warped, and the quicksilver in its mirror seemed weary now, and was so unquick you could scarcely see yourself in it. There was an old-fashioned basin atop the dresser, a Gideon Bible and a small electric fan. Yet, though the wooden walls seemed ancient, and the rug on the floor was threadbare in spots, everything was clean except the windows.

Mal mopped sweat with his already soaking-wet handkerchief, and for a moment wondered about the history of the room. Did it date back to the old days of Nevada? The outside of the building looked old enough to have originated in the eighties. And here in the room he felt like a character in a Western movie. If he looked out the window, would he see his horse tethered at the hitching post below? How many painted women of yore had contributed to bouncing the shape out of that mattress? How many lone gunmen had spent their last night on earth here? Were any babies born in that bed? How many people had died in it? The number of couples who had made love in it would be fantastic. No use speculating there. He was looking slowly around. A hotel room with a past. Then he tried to visualize Dee here. When the vision suddenly became very clear, he put the key in his pocket and left.

At a cocktail table back in Rainbow's End, he surprised the waitress by ordering a straight lemonade. Then, when he'd finished it, he decided that inasmuch as he had another hour or so before it was cool enough to go swimming, he'd take a nap. He left the casino and walked through heat that now was beginning gradually to diminish: it was almost bearable.

Inside the bungalow, he undressed, put on swimming trunks and stretched out on the bed. He heard the voice a few seconds later and at first thought it was his imagination. It was low, whispered—and intensely urgent:

"Mal, open the door, quickly. Please, *quickly!*"

He looked toward the window and saw Dee's face. Then he sprang up and rushed to the door and opened it and let her in before anyone could see her. That is, if someone hadn't *already.* He moved to the windows and shut the Venetian blinds tightly. Then he snapped on the bed lamp and turned around and looked at her. She had on white slacks and a green blouse and green sandals.

His stomach turned over. "Dee—what's the—why are you *here?*"

"I had to see you!"

"But, coming over here in—broad daylight!"

"Nobody saw me, Mal. I was careful."

"How'd you know which bungalow was mine?"

"I just now saw you walk in here."

He sat down on the bed and reached for a cigarette. His hands were shaking so hard he could scarcely get it out of the pack.

"I was warned—that unless I stayed away from you—"

"He warned *me,* too." Now she moved to him, took the cigarette pack, extracted one, put it between his lips, then flicked a flame from her lighter. "But if you're *this* scared, we'll call it off. Okay, Mal? It was crazy anyway. I'm very selfish to ask *anybody* to get mixed up in anything like this on my account. After all, it's no skin off *you.* I really had a nerve to even—"

"Shut up, Dee." He puffed at the cigarette.

"No, I'm serious. I don't want you to get hurt, I don't want *anybody* to get hurt. Thanks anyway, though. The thought was there—and that's what's important."

She started for the door. He jumped up, caught her arm. And in that awful moment something brand new hit him. Just the touch of her hand made him tingle. He let go of her, but now she was looking up into his face, waiting for him to say whatever he had intended to say.

He nodded. "Maybe we'd *better*—"

"Mal, what's the matter?"

He turned away. "I wish to God I knew!"

"So long."

Without facing her, he said harshly: "Look, I said we'd make a plan—work something out." He swung around now. "And that's what we're still going to do. Nothing's changed. I've already rented the room, in fact." He went over and picked up the hotel key. "Here's the key." He gave it to her but would not look at her. "It's tonight. Around 1:30 A.M.—right after my piano session."

He heard her say: "Not if you want to back out."

"I *don't* want to back out. But there's something else I have to tell you. Yesterday—when I met you at the dam— I was *told* to be there. My boss wanted it set up so he could bug Bello."

"Didn't you *want* to meet me?"

"Sure, but I wouldn't have. If he hadn't insisted, I'd have been too yellow to risk it."

"Is he *still* insisting?"

"No—now it's the other way around—like I told you. The new orders are to 'keep a country mile away from her.' " He pointed at the key she was holding. "Hotel Mammoth. It's old and sorry and hot. But a safer room to meet in than this one."

He at last met her eyes and found her studying his face.

She said: "Touch my hand again."

He touched it, then pulled away.

She said softly: "My real name is Diane."

"I like that better than Dee."

"Nobody's ever called me by my real name."

"May I?"

"Yes."

There was a silence between them.

She asked: "Am I looking at you in the same way?"

"How?"

"The way you're looking at me?"

"I don't know. Are you?"

"I think I am," she said.

"Crazy world." He was trying to throw it away.

"It certainly is."

"Be careful tonight, won't you? He may have someone following you."

She nodded. "I'll be careful. Don't worry. I'd better leave now."

"All right, I'll go outside, look around." He raised the Venetian blinds. "You watch—and when the coast is clear, I'll light a cigarette."

"Good."

Outside, it was still hot, and there was very little human traffic: but he checked everybody in sight. Then when he was sure it was safe, he lit the cigarette he'd brought with him. She slipped out of his bungalow and moved swiftly away. He watched her go.

He was trying not to think, or even feel.

Twenty-eight

4:42 P.M.

Joe was aware of a quiet commotion close to the table. The seedy player in the hunting shirt who had been in constant action since five this morning was showing signs of breaking completely. Like some kind of maniac, he was no longer rational. Eyes glazed, he continued to dig down, buy chips—which he lost within minutes. Twice he'd left the table, undoubtedly to get more money: and brought it back in large bills, even though he hadn't once approached the cashier's window. No ordinary man carries that much cash legitimately. You stand on the house side of the dice table and watch people's faces and you learn to judge them accurately. This man was a fugitive.

It didn't bother Joe that he was running from the law so much as it did that he was reaching a desperate state of shock which could turn into some form of violence. He was debating whether to warn Sprig when one of the waitresses from the coffee shop, an albino blonde, moved up to the man, touched his arm. She was apparently off duty because she wore a pale blue frock that accentuated the extreme milk-white of her skin.

"Everything all right, Si honey?" Her voice was anxious.

"Yeah—fine."

"We are leaving soon, aren't we?"

Shelby wasn't even listening. His eyes were on the dice table.

"You *said* we were."

"Anything I said—fine."

"When?"

"When what?"

"Are we leaving?"

"Any time now."

"I'll go pack then."

"Just *go*."

"I shall love it."

"Beat it, will you?"

"Hollywood!" She sighed.

He turned toward her. "If you don't get out of here—" His temples were throbbing; he looked like a madman. He choked back his anger. "If you don't get out of here," he repeated, "you won't be going anywhere."

"All right, dear, I'll be waiting for you." She walked off quickly.

Studying Shelby only a moment longer, Joe knew he had to ask Sprig to keep a watch on him. He moved away from the table—headed for the office. But Sprig wasn't there.

Rux sat at the desk and when he saw Joe seemed uneasy.

"Where's Sprig?" Joe asked.

"I—gosh, I don't know, Mr. Martin. Maybe he's corking off somewhere. He sure *needs* the sleep."

"You lying to me?"

"No—I—he didn't say exactly where he'd be."

"He always says exactly where he'll be."

"Probably so tired he just forgot."

Joe looked at Rux, then walked out. He glanced around the casino, and not seeing Sunny either, suddenly remembered he had noticed her start in the direction of the penthouse stairs some half hour ago. Probably to change into a swim suit, he'd decided then; it was getting toward the hour, on these sizzling days, when people finally came out to swim. She should have been down by now—and Sprig was on some mysterious errand! He squashed the cigarette he had just lit in a nearby ash stand and strode toward the stairs.

Sunny, wearing her bathing suit, sandals and a yellow toweling beach jacket, was backed against the wall of the penthouse, facing the tall, thoroughly exhausted Sprig, looking at the fury etched on his face, the deep, engulfing circles under his eyes. He had arrived shortly after she changed and it seemed now she had been facing him forever. He kept asking her endless, pointless, inane questions in the same, unchanging tired voice.

"You never knew anybody who lived in Las Vegas before?"

"No."

"You're sure?"

He didn't believe her. "Well, I—I come from a big family—" she started.

"Go on!"

"Go on—*what*?"

"And a few of the kids, your brothers and sisters, left home after they were of age and you're not sure where some of them went. Isn't that what you were going to say?"

A terror was growing in her. "How did you know?"

"So one or two of them *might have*—just might have—come to Las Vegas?"

She felt cold inside. "What are you getting at?"

"Maybe you didn't know about it until later."

"Know *what* until later?" she said desperately.

"About them living here."

He was weaving a web around her, putting words in her mouth.

"I—I don't know what it is you want me to say!"

"Yes, you do. Think now. You *do!*"

She was just staring at him as the door was flung open and Joe walked in. Relief surged through her; she wanted to run to him. But she was still, motionless. Sprig turned and the two men stood gazing at one another knowing now there was real trouble between them and that it was irrevocable.

"What'd you learn?" Joe's rage was so great he could scarcely get the words out.

"Nothing," Sprig said, *"yet."*

"Sunny, has he—touched you—laid a hand on you?"

"No."

"He has a way of shaking a woman when he wants her to talk. It always works. He knows every trick there is." He was looking at Sprig again. "But he doesn't understand people. Sunny, do you have anything you want to tell him?"

She saw that Joe was in almost a trance. "Joe, he—he was very *polite* to me. Please, it's all right!"

"Go downstairs."

"Joe!"

"Go on!"

She left hurriedly.

Joe said: "If you'd shaken her she would have talked. Just like a Mama doll. The harder you shook her the more she'd repeat it: *'I love Joe. I love Joe.'* " There was agony on Joe's face. "Too bad you didn't shake her and get that confession. Yes, to use your words, that's the Wop I was up here humping last midnight. You couldn't leave her alone, could you? You had to pry into my private life. The best private and *most* private life I've had since the day I was born!"

He hit Sprig now, sent him sprawling back. The lanky security man made no effort to fight. Joe approached, pulled him in close and hit him again. A trickle of blood seeped out the corner of Sprig's mouth. Sprig—whom Joe knew to be one of the toughest human beings on the face of the earth. He could probably break Joe in two, and still there was no fight in him. Joe wanted to hit him again, but couldn't.

"Get out of here—out of the casino—off the premises. You're fired!"

Sprig shook his head. "Like most of the other employees, I own stock here, stock you made us buy so we'd all be co-owners. All of us partners together. So you can't fire me—at least not until this siege is over. I'm staying on—to protect my interest." Then he added, "Partner."

"You heard me, Sprig—get your ass out of Rainbow's End—now!"

"No. I'm going to continue working for you whether you want me to or not."

"Badgering the girl I'm in love with? *That's* working for me?" Joe was conscious that he had said aloud to someone besides Sunny that he loved her.

"Joe—I don't say she isn't everything you think she is— she could have been roped into some kind of a deal— didn't know what the hell she was doing—"

"She wasn't roped into anything!"

"Maybe not." Sprig's voice was dead. "But I'm paid to

check on everything—every angle. And that's what I was doing."

Joe stood there; he was leaden. Sprig moved past him, hand on his jaw, and went out.

He walked down the stairs from the penthouse feeling worse than he had ever felt at any time in his life. In the casino, he moved toward the office, and went in.

Rux looked at him, saw the bloody mouth.

"*I* didn't tell him you were up there."

"No, the man's uncanny, that's all. Let me sit down."

Rux got up and Sprig sat in the swivel chair. He leaned forward on the desk, putting his hand to his forehead. There was pain all over him.

"He actually hit you, huh?"

"Yeah—he actually did."

"Doesn't he know you're the best man he's ever—"

"Yeah, he knows."

"You going to take it?"

"I took it."

Rux fell silent.

Sprig leaned back, looking at the ceiling. "I feel awful. I feel like hell! Will you go out and leave me alone for a while, Rux?"

"Sure."

Twenty-nine

An airline round trip for two to Las Vegas from Los Angeles will cost between sixty and eighty dollars, a first-class hotel room fifteen, dinner for two ten; cocktails average seventy-five cents each. Yet, under "business announcements," the classified ad section of newspapers in this city offer:

VISIT
Fabulous
LAS VEGAS

3 days & 2 nights
$25.00
(per person)
Choice of Strip Hotel
Luxury Room, 2 nites
Cocktail & Dinner at
Another Hotel with
$10 per couple
TO SPEND
Cocktails at 3rd Spot
Golf and Swimming.
HO. 3000

The ten dollars "to spend" is in the form of white chits of paper, worth one dollar each in Las Vegas only, and not exchangeable for either money or chips. A person using them in a blackjack game or at a crap table usually feels self-conscious, and then secretly glad when he's lost the last of them. Las Vegas is also glad, because that's where the gimmick of the bargain offer begins to work: when the customer reaches into his wallet for money.

It was almost five-thirty, and Mal, wearing bathing trunks, a towel over his shoulder, his feet pushed into beach sandals, was just leaving his bungalow when the telephone rang. He stepped back inside, answered. It was Shelby, his voice urgent:

"Krazycat, buddy, I've got to talk to you. It's important."

"Later," Mal said.

"*Later?* Listen—I'm wiped out!"

"I'm sorry to hear—"

"Don't give me that crap you're sorry. You're with them. You told me if I followed Bello's bets—"

"Look, you son of a bitch—"

Shelby's voice was contrite now. "Krazycat—I was just blowing off steam. I'm a little excited. I've wired to California for money. It'll be here tomorrow. Meantime, how about a geeola? I'll pay you back as soon as—"

"A thousand dollars?" Mal said. "Are you nuts? I don't keep that kind of dough."

"You can get it—you work here. The cashier'll give it to you."

"Won't the cashier give it to you? You're a business-man. You can write checks."

"I haven't established credit yet."

"Well, I don't have it," Mal said. "My salary goes to my business manager every week and he just gives me so much to live on."

"You Hollywood bastards!" Shelby rasped. "Business managers!"

"I'm on my way to go swimming," Mal told him. "See you around."

He hoped he wouldn't, but when he crawled out of the water twenty minutes later, Si Shelby was sitting tensely in a sloped-back canvas deck chair as close to the edge of the pool as he could get. Mal shook his head to flick water off, and the smoldering late afternoon sun, still breathtak-ingly hot, absorbed most of the rest almost immediately.

"Looking for me?"

"Krazycat, I've got to have that G—just until morning!"

Mal sat down on the tile. "I told you—I don't have it, can't get it."

"Jesus, you must have *some* money!"

"I've got a hundred I was going to play around with."

"A *hundred?* A lousy, stinking hundred dollars?"

"Yeah—you see, I'm not a big man like you."

Shelby looked at him long and hard. "Listen, I'll tell you what kind of a jam I'm in—I'll level with you. Then maybe you'll spring for more than just a measly hundred bucks."

"Why should I spring for anything?" Mal snapped, "I'm no kin to you."

"Listen, just listen, will you? Things went to hell for me in the car business. It was coming for a long time—"

"Shelby—I don't want to hear about it."

"My wife left me eight or ten months ago—Tijuana divorce. Cutest doll you've ever seen. She used to be a cigarette girl in a night club. Only she had a bad personal smash-up of some kind—busted romance. And she was pretty sad when I married her. But she was so terrific looking, I didn't care—and we hit everything off fine."

"Will you get to the point—if there *is* one?"

But Si Shelby took his time, suffering inwardly. "It was fine, just fine; I made her forget the other romance; but I'd been married twice before and had three kids by one and one by the other—and these two ex-wives kept giving me a bad time: eating up my money; and finally I began drinking a little, and dating bar tarts now and then, and Mildred caught me a few times. Mildred is the ex-cigarette girl. I guess she caught me one time too many. Anyway, she took off."

"Which is what I'm going to do," Mal said, "if you don't get to the point." And he thought of Mildred, who-ever she was, and wherever she was—with one more busted romance on her hands. Ex-Mrs. Shelby the third. Maybe she was back peddling cigarettes; or maybe she had just lain down and died.

"So being a bachelor again, I played around a lot—spent too much dough—" He saw the boredom in Mal's eyes and cut it short. "I chiseled on some pink slips to the cars—got them from a wholesaler—floored them with both a bank and a finance company—the *same* cars—and left town with eleven thousand dollars that wasn't mine."

"Is the law after you?"

"I don't think so, not yet. The bank, the wholesaler

and the finance company'll be snarled up for weeks, each claiming ownership of the cars. They may swear out warrants later, but even so, somebody told me it's hard to reach across a state line on an embezzlement rap."

"Don't kid yourself."

Shelby reddened. The splash of water, laughter and excited voices echoed from the pool. A blonde stretched herself out on the lawn not ten feet away.

"You trying to scare me, Krazycat?"

"No, they pick them up every day, and Nevada is happy to sign the extradition papers."

"Quit needling me!"

"I'm not," Mal told him quietly. "For a man who's just turned crooked, you're awfully naive. I'll bet your real name *is* Shelby, isn't it?"

"Sure it is." Shelby was taut now. "Look, cut it out; cut this stuff out."

"Did you really believe you could steal from all those different people and wriggle out of it by merely crossing a state line?"

"Nobody's come near me so far!"

"As you say, it takes time to swear out the warrants; but I bet they know where you are."

The blonde lying on the lawn was joined by a middle-aged man and two children in their teens. They sat down around her, cross-legged; then the four of them talked to one another in soft pleasant voices. They seemed happy and very relaxed.

"Think so?" Shelby was tense, his body stiffening; veins bulged at his neck.

"Wouldn't be hard to guess, would it?" Mal said. "You came to the obvious place."

"All right," Shelby cut in harshly, desperately; the blonde and one of the children looked over. "But what about getting me some dough? I've leveled with you, told you the whole thing—"

"And before that," Mal reminded him, "you said you had money coming tomorrow. But when you realized you couldn't steal from me, you decided to beg!"

"Look, just let me have a thousand and I'll get it back so fast—"

"How? How'll you get it back?"

"Never mind. I have a way."

"So does everybody who comes to Las Vegas. You've already dropped eleven thousand dollars of other people's money, but you're not adding a thousand of mine to it."

Shelby's face was crestfallen, panicky. "You mean you're going to let me down?"

"You let your brokenhearted wife Mildred down, didn't you?" Mal's voice was just above a whisper, but very intense. "And your other two wives, and your four children; you were even going to let *me* down a thousand dollars worth if you could swing it."

"How much *will* you give me, then? Will you give me *anything?*"

"The hundred we talked about. Use it to pay your hotel and food bill. Then check out." Mal climbed to his feet.

Shelby stood now, too, and looked worse standing up: He seemed almost falling to pieces. "Can I go to your bungalow with you and get the hundred?"

"No. I'll see you in the casino."

"When?"

"Half an hour or so."

When he entered the casino forty-five minutes later, Shelby was waiting. He motioned him away, then walked over to the cashier and got a hundred dollar bill by signing a chit. When he turned around, he saw that Shelby was no longer alone. Cottontop had joined him, her very white face so flushed with relief she was nearly crying, and she more than ever resembled a kind of cute scarecrow: or a flippy-floppy rag doll with white braid hair. Mal strolled over to them.

"Oh, honey," Cottontop was saying, "I've tried to reach you everywhere! But here you are at last, dear. I'm all packed and ready. Quit my job this morning. Are we leaving for Hollywood soon?"

"Look," Shelby said irritably, "get lost."

"Get *lost?* Dear, what do you mean by that?"

"I MEAN GET THE HELL LOST!"

Cottontop was horror-struck, and several people turned around, staring at them.

"Tell her the truth," Mal said.

"Stay out of this, Krazycat!"

"The truth about what?" Cottontop asked. "Please! The truth about *what?*"

"I tried to tell you at the piano before this started."

But she didn't look at him or hear him; she was clutching Shelby's sleeve. "The truth about what?"

"The truth about nothing," Shelby snapped. He was embarrassed. "Just go away, will you, you're attracting attention."

"Either you tell her or you don't get this C-note," Mal threatened.

Shelby looked at the hundred dollar bill, then said to Cottontop: "I'm not a talent scout. I'm no part of the movies. I'm a used car dealer."

The little waitress was numb with shock. It was a moment before she could speak; then, giddy with a truth she couldn't accept, she said: "Oh, I know. I know! This is a joke. You and Mr. Davis made it up together. Oh, what a good practical joker you are, honey! Very convincing.

That's the way people in Hollywood do, don't they? Everything's a joke."

"It's no joke," Mal said.

She looked at him. "I told him about The Home. You know, that orphanage in Nebraska."

"I didn't know anything about it," Mal said.

Cottontop was swaying very slightly from side to side. "How nobody would ever adopt me because I look so odd —I'm so white all over." She turned back to Shelby. "And you said it was probably because I was too unusual, but being unusual was what would make me a star." She returned her gaze to Mal. "There were no movies there, or TV, either. I didn't see one single movie until they let me out—and I was eighteen by then. But, oh, did I make up for lost time! I became a *student* of Hollywood—kept files with the name of every star; then I started a list of every actor, no matter how small his part was—like—like when *you* played in a movie once. Oh, I don't mean to be disrespectful, you had a *fine* part, but—" Her voice ran down, and then she said: "Did he lie to me?"

"Yeah, Cindy, he did."

"But how could he?" Her face began to break. She looked at Shelby: and there was almost nothing left of him. He was pasty, sweating. "How *could* you, honey? I— I told you I was a virgin. I *asked* you to wait. Oh, I was terribly drunk—I've never been drunk like that—but I remember asking you—"

"Will you shut up!"

"No, I won't shut up."

"Lower your voice then," Shelby demanded.

"I won't do that, either," said Cottontop. "I told you, I warned you, I begged—but you wouldn't listen—and you were so filthy, so—" She began to sob uncontrollably, and a uniformed casino policeman, alerted by the sound, headed over. "You were so— How could you? How could *anybody* be so—"

The policeman arrived, and Mal said: "Take her to Joe's office, will you?"

A small crowd had begun to gather, and the cop led Cottontop gently away, still crying loudly. Shelby had taken all he could without collapsing and didn't care about the people who remained, watching the two of them.

"Have I earned that hundred dollars yet?"

"Sure," Mal said. He handed it to him.

Thirty

When Mal entered the office, Cottontop was on the floor, sobbing loudly, beating her fists into the cushions on one of the divans; she seemed almost in a spasm of pain. Sprig was watching, bewildered. The casino policeman nodded at Mal, his eyes eager. "We all like this kid," he said. "What'd he do to her?"

"Better get back outside," Sprig told him curtly.

As the cop went out, Mal said: "I'll tell you about it some other time."

"Tell *me* about it," Sprig invited.

"When Joe gets here."

"You've sent for him?"

"Yeah."

There was a peculiar look on Sprig's face. "I guess *he* can take care of it then—whatever it is. See you later."

Mal gaped as Sprig closed the door behind him. Bad blood between Sprig and Joe? It was too incredible to believe.

Cottontop was still sobbing, and he tried to pick her

up now, but she fought him off, flailing her arms. "Leave me alone! Just leave me alone! I'm going to kill myself!" As he backed away, she swung her body around, still sitting on the floor by the divan, her face streaked with tears and blobs of mascara, her hair disarrayed; she was biting her lips. Her breath was short, fast. "He was going to take me to Hollywood. HOLLYWOOD!" The crying started again now, worse than ever, and she crawled into the middle of the room, beating soundlessly on the thick, black rug.

"Cindy, listen to me. Joe'll be here in a minute. Do you want him to see you looking like this?"

She went on crying, but allowed Mal to lift her to her feet. Even burdened with such heavy grief, she was light as a blade of grass: a skinny little thing, not much to her. The door opened and Joe came in. She saw him, and tried to calm herself somewhat: she had a terrible respect for anybody in authority. Mal helped her onto a divan, and she sat there crying softly. Joe looked at her. He seemed almost irritated.

"What's the matter?"

Mal said: "She was manhandled by a phony who said he was going to take her to Hollywood. Even quit her job."

"Where is the guy?"

"It was a pretty bad scene out there. I imagine he's hit the road. He's a go-broke."

Joe walked over to Cottontop and sat down beside her, and Mal was surprised at the gentleness in his tone. "Take it easy, kitten; the world hasn't ended yet. Maybe that phony jerk doesn't want you, but we do."

Cottontop tried to subdue the little sobs that kept welling up in her throat. "Please don't say that because I know it isn't true; nothing is any more, nothing is true. It's very nice of you, sir, but—"

"It is true," Joe said. "You see me tomorrow morning.

I'll put you on temporarily as a shill; and the first waitress job that opens up is yours. Hell, it might even be in the casino where the main-line action is instead of that unexciting coffee shop."

Mal continued to be amazed: Joe knew just how to talk to her, exactly what to say; when he wanted to turn it on, this man had real charm. Cottontop had suddenly stopped crying entirely.

"You mean it?"

"Of course I mean it."

Mal added: "Cindy, baby, *everybody* wants you to stay here, all the employees."

She stared at both of them, the tears drying in her eyes. "You don't think bad of me?"

"We love you," Joe said softly. "You're our little character." He climbed to his feet.

She got up then, too. "Thank you, Mr. Martin." She moved to a mirror on the wall and hastily began repairing her face. "I appreciate it very much. I really do appreciate it more than you'll ever know."

"Need any money to tide you over?" Joe asked.

She turned from the mirror, making last touches at her hair. "Oh, no, sir; I save my money. I have quite a bit put away. It's in the bank."

"Good for you."

That's irony, Mal thought, if Shelby had known about her savings, he would have conned her a little harder, been nicer to her a little longer—piled lie on top of lie, and eventually would have had every penny of it. He looked over at Joe.

"There have been times," he said, "when I thought you were solid iron."

Joe grinned faintly. "I'm almost as human as you."

"Now you're going too far! How's Sunny?"

"She's fine."

"Pretty fond of her, aren't you?"

"Does it show?"

"Just on the edges." He paused. "Anything wrong between you and Sprig?"

Joe sobered. "*He* say there was?"

"No, he just—I don't know."

"Mind your own business." His voice was hard now, and he was frowning. "I have to get back to the game."

"How is the game, Joe? Is Bello into you for very much?"

"Nearly two million."

There was something in the way Joe said it that startled Mal, and then touched him: two million in the hole, and he'd taken time out to comfort a coffee shop waitress.

A few minutes later, he was moving through the casino when Kiki caught up with him.

"Mal—"

He turned, faced the long-legged showgirl, and for some reason he couldn't understand seemed to flush with guilt. He hadn't called her or seen her in the past couple of days, but he could alibi around that. Instead, he just stood here, flat-footed.

"Hi."

She said: "That's what I wanted to know."

"What?"

She told him softly: "I read eyes."

"And what are mine saying?"

"Goodbye."

"Hey now—whoa—aren't you jumping to wild conclusions?"

She seemed sad. "Am I?"

Her honesty withered him. "Kid, listen—"

She shook her head. "No, ever since the other night when we did the town and you were in that funny, low mood—I knew it was just about the end between us."

"You amaze me."

"I amaze myself," she said, "the mistakes I make: like
thinking that I was your girl."

There was no use trying to lie to her. All he said was:
"You came close."

"I doubt that, Mal."

She turned, hurried away now, and Mal stood there,
fumbling for a cigarette, and somehow shaken. Yet he was
grateful she had let him out so easy, and remembered
times when it hadn't been that easy—and then finally
that one particular time in Palm Springs with Nina, who
had spent two weeks there, most of it with him.

The place was called The Sunrise and he had played
piano there for the season, not drawing a really sober
breath in three whole months; but then, nobody else did
either, so it seemed like the way to live; they'd had a crowd
that just wouldn't stop, stayed on and on—all of them
rich, except for some of the women on the fringe who
floated in and out, and always remained as long as they
could. Whit, who owned the place, was as bad as the rest,
and richer than any of them. He was the one who started
pushing people into the pool with their clothes on, and
after that everybody took it up, so that it wasn't safe to go
near the water unless you were ready to swim. The first
time Mal got pushed in he was fully dressed and holding
a highball glass in his hand which splintered on the side
and cut his face; everybody had laughed, and so did he
after he climbed out, but he still carried a small scar at
the tip of his nose to show that he had been there and
lived through those days. The nights, of course, had been
fabulous; he had real attention when he was at the piano.

But Nina hadn't belonged with that giddy-rich crowd,
though at the time he had imagined just the opposite.
She was a secretary for a firm in Portland, Oregon, and
saved her money ever year to spend a two-week vacation

in some glamorous resort. First it was Cuba, she'd told him, then New York, New Orleans and Sun Valley, Idaho. She was a tall, pretty girl with a dark complexion and long hair that she wore in a bun. When she unfastened it, it was halfway down her back: shiny, glistening black, and soft as silk. She was serious, but he hadn't realized it until the last day when it was too late; so he'd seen her off on the Greyhound bus, and promised to write, telling her she could always reach him through his booking agency, and she wrote a couple of letters that he didn't answer, and then a whole year later he got a postcard from Mexico City on which she had written, "Having a *wonderful* time on my vacation. And I don't miss you one bit" and he thought it was sort of funny that she was so bitter, but a year after that a card came from Honolulu with the same message and he didn't think it was funny any more. The last card reached him a month ago from Miami, Florida, and this time the message was different. It said: "Was married yesterday. Ha. Ha."

It was always during the best times of your life that the worst things happened.

But Kiki wasn't the type who would send him a card saying: "Just got married. Ha, ha." She was a showgirl and a little more brittle than a secretary with long black hair down her back. Or was she? Was any woman really brittle?

He moved on through the casino now, trying to forget all the times he had loved when it wasn't love; and all at once, as though the subject was related to this, he began to think of Dee, of Bello. What was the big plan they would devise to pull her away from him? Gently—without bloodshed? He stared at Bello, who was standing at the dice table: and all at once realized what he must have known all along. There *wasn't* any way to pry Dee from him without some kind of bloodshed.

Thirty-one

11:23 P.M.

It was an old church, and small, yet its worn wooden floors had felt the soft, wet touch of more tear drops than many larger places of worship; it had heard wailing within its thin walls, and had known every human anguish ever suffered. It stood here on a dirty street, its own edifice streaked from rain and weather; yet it was cloaked in a quiet, pious dignity—and its doors were never closed: for the great tragedies and the small ones know no time or hour in Las Vegas. The need for solace is a continuous one.

It was dark, though; in total darkness save for the nickering candlelight at the feet of the images of saints. Dark and empty and silent—until the front door pushed open and the lamplight from the street silhouetted the figure of a young woman. She moved slowly forward, the door closing behind her, dropped to one knee, crossing herself before the altar, then groped past rows of seats on the outside aisle until she reached the statue of the Virgin.

Now Sunny's face was visible in the tiny lights of candles as she threw herself to her knees, crying in anguish, knowing a torment so great that she could not cope with it alone.

After the scene with Sprig, she had been unable to talk to Joe. He had returned to the dice table, and she knew that nothing must disturb him while he was there. Anyway, to tell him the truth while the game was in progress could demoralize and ruin him. He probably wouldn't be able to concentrate any more—might not want to, might not *care*—and it'd be her fault. All of it would be her fault.

Later, when the game was ended and Bello was gone, she could explain: how certain men had been planted in the casino to watch Joe, watch his every move, weeks and months before the big game started. They had been instructed to look for weak spots. And then, in the midst of that, *she* had arrived on that free weekend. They'd noticed her, but hadn't paid much attention, until she returned the following week and Joe took her for a boat ride on Lake Mead.

She hadn't intended going back ever again after that. For one thing, she couldn't afford it. But then a "Mr. Wily" had appeared at her house in San Francisco, and introduced himself. He wore horn-rimmed glasses, looked businesslike; his voice had been pleasant, convincing. He was there, in her father's house, saying how somebody had noticed Sunny, found out her name: and then had connected her with a boy named Al Guido who'd disappeared three years ago. Al, her brother, a bum, but still her brother, messing around on the fringe of Las Vegas. "They found him face down in the sand," Wily had said, "eight bullet holes through his chest. The police never solved the case, but I know who killed him. Not the punk who fired the bullets but the big shot who hired him to do it. Joe Martin—Mr. Joe Martin himself. And for one reason only: he didn't like the kid." There had been great shouting in her father's house that night: a storm that had lasted until daylight. "You can't prove it," Wily had said, "you won't even be able to get close to him if you go up there. He has a human screen around him—men who guard him." But her father swore he'd try and the next morning he bought a gun.

Wily was waiting that afternoon when Sunny left the school. He was worried about her father, he said; if the old man tried to tackle Joe Martin, he'd probably end up in the desert like his son Al. Now if he could promise him that someone else would take care of the job—somebody more experienced....

"Who?" she had asked.

"You." And he had gone into long detail then. Murder is a cardinal sin. But Al's death could be avenged. And Joe's punishment could be meted to him another way: by losing his wealth, his power, his casino. Surely, then, on the way down, some little hoodlum would finish him off. A giant move was on to strip Joe of his worldly possessions and she could help.

All she had to do was spend a few more weekends at the casino and make him notice her. She was an offbeat girl for him, the only kind who might tempt him—a "decent girl" were Wily's words. If she managed to get his attention when the "big operation" started, he'd be distracted and even if it was only a minor distraction, it would help. They wanted his mind to be on something besides dice. They'd do the rest.

She had refused the proposition at first, but that night when she realized that only Wily could deter her father from trying to kill Joe Martin, she changed her mind; she agreed on the stipulation that her father wasn't to know, because he would never have permitted it. To him she was his baby daughter who had to be sheltered.

Wily had paid her expenses after that. She wasn't required to see him again, nor to make reports to anyone. She was not a spy in any sense, just a "distraction."

Her face lifted to the image of the Blessed Virgin above her and she whispered: "He'll understand. He loves me and he'll understand when I tell him. He'll remember how, after that night in his office when he kissed me and I felt such a terrible attraction for him, I wanted to leave the next morning. He'll remember that I *tried* to leave—tried to run away. But he said he needed me and when he said that I believed him, and I believed I could help him,

and that's what I've tried to do. I've tried to help him
every time. Because would I hurt the one and only man
I've ever loved? Would I do that? And last night, when he
left the game to be near me, I nearly fought with him to
make him go back to the dice. He'll remember that, too,
and all the other things. And eventually, he'll even be glad
Wily sent me, that it happened the way it did, because
otherwise we would never have seen each other again.

"He'll realize I know a lot more now than I did that
day Wily showed up at our house. That I have since then
recognized his deceit. Because Joe *couldn't* have killed
Al. It was just that the syndicate, or whoever it was, chose
me because Joe liked me, then went to great bother to
look up my family history and *invented* the story of Al's
death. For all we know, Al may still be alive somewhere
—roaming the world. Joe can't hate me (*can* he hate me?)
because I was fool enough to believe all that?"

Yet her tears were unchecked.

She returned to Rainbow's End shortly after midnight,
and heard herself being paged on the loudspeaker. She
hurried over to the desk, and found Joe standing there.

"Where have you been?"

She glanced around, didn't see Bello. "Is the game
over?"

"No. Bello wants a break. One hour. Food time. And
maybe a catnap."

She tried to smile but her face felt wooden. "Last midnight it was *you*."

"This midnight it's Bello and me. Come on."

"Where we going?"

"You'll see." He led her outside.

"Were you waiting for me long?"

"Five minutes," he said. "Seemed like eternity."

"I went to church."

"Why?"

"Felt like it."

"Is anything bothering you?"

"No."

They reached his car, and he held the door open. She repeated: "Where are we going, Joe?"

"A luau."

"In Las Vegas?"

"I made special arrangements."

"We will be back in an hour?"

"On the dot," he said. They got in and he was backing the car. Now they moved forward. "The dice turned to ice these past few hours." She didn't understand the term and he explained: "When they're cold, the house wins. I'm the house." They were on the highway now, the lights shining directly ahead. "Had me winging for two million."

"Two million!"

"It's down to one million five. Million and a half," he added, reading puzzlement on her face.

"A million and a half dollars," she breathed, trying to comprehend that figure. "A million and a half dollars and you want to go to a luau?!"

"It's all right—long as Bello's gone, too."

"How can you even think of *anything* except losing that much money?"

"It's easy."

"What happened between you and Mr. Sprig?"

"He won't bother you again." But she'd touched a raw nerve. "Why *did* you go to church?"

"I often go on weeknights." That wasn't true. She did sometimes go on weeknights but the times were not often.

"Oh."

"Won't you tell me where the luau is?" It was safer to change the subject.

"Lake Mead."

"How many people will be there?"

"Two."

Even in the moonlight, she recognized landmarks and minutes before they got there guessed he was taking her to the same cove where they'd been yesterday. But when they arrived, when he parked just off the road and helped her out onto the soft earth, she felt a surge of disappointment.

"Someone is there," she said. "They've built a fire."

"Whoever is there will have to leave," he told her softly. "Come on."

The fire glow grew brighter as they approached; it flickered against the night sky like the flames from a small volcano and when, finally, they came to the rocky wall of the cove, she imagined she could feel its angry, red heat. They reached the opening and she stopped in amazed wonderment.

The cove lay revealed before them, a circle of sand bounded by the lake on one side and rough-hewn rocks on the other, and against the rocks, thrust into the sand, were a dozen torches on metal sticks. The sand flickered gold and crimson in their fitful flare and the still water of the lake glowed with rainbow ripples.

Several cushions were heaped on the sand; beside them stood a silver champagne bucket and a picnic basket.

"If you ask in the right way," Joe said, "Rainbow's End will arrange almost anything. They use those torches in Hawaii—at Waikiki. Like it?"

"It's beautiful," she said.

"I don't know about you, bambino, but I'm starved." He flopped down on a cushion, reached for the hamper.

But she hurried over, pulled his fingers away. "Just sit there," she said, "I'll serve you."

"Slave girl."

"Yes, darling. That's me."

There was cold turkey and potato salad and olives and

vegetables in aspic. She spooned this out on blue plastic plates.

"Midnight luau," he said. "Only there's no roast pig or poi; and we have champagne instead of okoolehow."

"Okoolehow?"

"Something the Hawaiians drink. It gives them a fat belly." He was eating now.

"You must have planned all this hours ago."

"No—I was thinking of us at Waikiki—and then decided—why wait? You recognize where we are, don't you?"

"Yes, darling, the moment we got here."

"I ought to build a fence around this spot and preserve it forever."

"Joe, do you know I adore you?"

"Say it again."

"I adore you!"

"Which reminds me why I brought you here."

"Why?"

"Because I adore you, too."

"Oh—is *that* why?"

"No, there's another reason." He set his empty plate down on the sand. "Something I want to ask you."

She shivered, because it was coming now, she could feel it: Sprig's suspicion had kindled one in Joe. And when he asked her point-blank, she wouldn't be able to lie, to conceal anything from him.

"Go ahead," she whispered, "ask."

"Will you marry me?"

This was all he wanted to know? There was no suspicion in him toward her—only trust? She began to cry again, and he pushed her gently down, kissing away the tears, then kissing her mouth.

Thirty-two

1:40 A.M.

Mal reached the second floor of the Hotel Mammoth ten minutes late. Though there was no light under the door of room 203, he felt she was inside. Eagerly, he tried the knob. It wouldn't turn. He spoke softly: "Dee." There was no answer. He waited impatiently, then realized that speaking one word didn't completely identify him. "Dee, it's Mal. Diane, open the door." No sound from inside. He stood there in the hall, feeling foolish, desolate.

After a few moments, he began to walk up and down the corridor. A couple passed him and he pretended to be on his way somewhere. Once they were inside their room, he returned to 203, took off his shoes and resumed pacing the corridor silently. He smoked one cigarette on top of another. His thoughts were like fireworks, off in all directions; and he found himself catching for breath—sucking deeply to get air into his lungs. Where is she? *Where is she?*

Time went on, *on* and on, the minutes crawling. He lit a match and checked his wristwatch a dozen times. Then he ran out of matches and couldn't even light a cigarette; but he continued checking his watch in the moonlight on the fire escape at the rear of the hall. At two he knew she wasn't coming. Maybe she had been followed. Maybe Bello suspected. She isn't going to show up! That's the thing, isn't it? She won't be here. Diane won't be here. So why don't you go back to Rainbow's End and load up on drinks and forget this? But he couldn't leave.

At fifteen after two he heard someone on the steps.

Just another tenant, he told himself, some weary dame who's lost her week's pay on the slot machines. But he watched the stairs avidly, and when Dee appeared, couldn't even move. She stared at him for a moment in the dim light.

"Mal," she whispered, "why you—you look terrible!"

She unlocked the door of 203, and they went inside. He walked to the window that faced the street, refusing even to look at her until he had regained control of himself. He felt utterly stupid and helpless. But presently he relaxed and turned around, conscious now that he was still in his stocking feet.

She was at the door, her back to it. In black slacks and a dark blouse, she was like an exotic little peasant.

At last she said: "I'm afraid in here."

"You're being followed?"

"Nobody followed me, but I'm afraid. He has the syndicate on his side—big men and hundreds of little men. I don't want to be trapped in a room like—"

"You won't be trapped. We won't be here very long."

"Mal, I'm so afraid, I feel as if I'm dying of fright."

"You won't feel that way after tonight."

"You have a plan?"

"Yes."

His own fear was receding now—thank God it was receding; he was icy cold and resolved.

"I'll do whatever you say—except—"

"There can be no exceptions. No arguments." She was suddenly frightened anew, trying to read his eyes, to jump ahead and decipher what he was going to say before he said it. "There's only one thing that'll make Bello cut you free—so that you'll *really* be free—where he'll never molest you again."

"What?"

"His pride."

"But how are we—"

"That's his only concern. What *other* people think of him. Almost *anything* he says or does in public—particularly in a casino, becomes famous."

"Yes, I *know*, Mal, but—"

"So if somebody tells him in front of a room full of people that his girl wants to leave him—"

She grew pale. "Who's going to do that?"

"I am. And since he'll want to keep face, there isn't a damn thing he can do but let you go."

"Wait a minute." She stared at him. "*You're* going to tell him that I want out?"

He nodded. "Over that portable microphone that I sing into—so it'll be loud and clear. To make it sound good, I'll have to embellish it a little. Like saying that you're in love with me. That's a lie, but it doesn't matter—as long as it works."

There was silence now, and she was staring at him, her beauty never greater than at this moment: the exquisite and fragile angelic-waif face.

"You *know* I can't let you do that."

He said: "I've thought and thought and it's the only possible way."

"He'd kill you."

"I don't think so."

"He'd certainly do *something* to you. Do you think he'd just forget it?"

"You asked me to help you—I was the one you chose. Remember?"

"But I'm not going to let you be hurt. Why, to even consider such a thing you must be—" She stopped.

"Don't say it."

She was studying him. "I was going to say 'crazy,' but it isn't that at all, is it?"

"No, I know the risk. I'm not crazy."

She said slowly: "It's—but you *couldn't!*"

"Couldn't what?"

She avoided the direct answer. "Tell me something. Think. *Why* does a girl choose a certain man to ask for help? One man above all others—and put her trust in him?"

"He reminds her of her father?"

"No. Try again."

"We're way off the subject, Diane."

"No, we aren't. I'm not going to let you go through with it. But if you *did* tell Bello I was in love with you, it *wouldn't* be a lie." She rushed on: "And you wouldn't offer yourself up on a chopping block unless you—unless you felt the very same way!"

He felt numb all over now, and this old room where Wyatt Earp and all the others had once slept was suddenly so close it was suffocating. He saw Dee only through a haze of pain and longing.

"You don't know what you're saying. You're beautiful —only twenty years old—the whole world's in front of you."

Tears glistened in her uptilted green eyes. "Didn't you hear me? I said I'm in love with you."

He shook his head. "I'm not going to let you make two mistakes in your life." He had to be sure this time. Sure of himself, of her. Love was too rare a thing to just jump at, or guess at.

"It *isn't* a mistake!"

"We'll get you out of this mess with Bello, then you can decide who and what you want.

"I want *you!*"

"No."

"*Yes.*" She started unbuttoning her blouse. "I'll *prove* that I want you."

He caught her hand. "Not that way."

"I don't know any other way."

"Not until you're free. Not until it's right. *Will* you let me tell him tonight?"

"If you say you love me."

"I love you, Diane!"

"Then we'll face him together—and take whatever he has to dish out—together. I'm that brave if you are. Are you that brave?"

He gazed at her and whispered: "Just this once in my life."

And they were in each other's arms then, kissing.

Thirty-three

"…Seven a winner. Pay the front line. Coming out again. It's betting time. Ee-o-leven! A natural. Pay the line. He's rolling them again. Take the odds on craps and eleven. Here they go!—Seven! Seven wins it again. Hop onto this hot shooter. Make your bets, please. Five, five a number. Now place your come and field bets. Man's looking for a five. Nine, the number is five…"

It was 3:10 A.M. The play was heavy at every table in the room, the slot machines jangled ceaselessly; the mixer behind the cocktail bar buzzed almost every other minute; pretty waitresses wearing leather skirts and short cowboy boots slipped in and out with trays of free drinks for the customers who were gambling. Three-ten in the morning and Mal was at the piano. The fear was all through him now. It was a living thing in his stomach like a spasm of unendurable pain. His forehead was specked with sweat, and he was playing badly—and could scarcely sing at all. His voice sounded squeaky. Maybe he should postpone it all until tomorrow. No, no, if you postpone it now, you'll never go through with it. You want to postpone it because you're so afraid. He *was* afraid, and the fear was getting bigger all the time. He wanted to go somewhere and try and retch it up out of his stomach. He wanted to cry out against the savage pain of it. You're not so brave *now,* are you? It's nearly time when you should signal her, but you can't; you're going to quail; you're too scared—you're going to funk out. She's glanced at you twice. She's waiting. And if you don't hurry up, the regular trio that plays at this hour will be back from intermission.

Suddenly Bello turned and was looking at him; his coal-black hair glistened with pomade, and the graying sideburns gave the heavy features a certain distinction. No mistaking, this was a big, big man; and his dead, cold expression seemed to throw down a gauntlet. Without a word, he left the crap table and started over. He was wearing a charcoal-gray suit, as usual, with a gray semi-sports shirt, open at the collar. It was his uniform. He stepped up to the higher level where the piano was.

Mal's fingers froze on the keys, and Dee, at the table which Bello had left, stared unbelievingly. Joe watched, and even the stickman was looking up, his eyes no longer on the precious chips. All six of the piano high stools were filled, but Bello edged his way between two people, flipped over a hundred dollar chip that landed on the piano keys.

"Play *My Melancholy Baby.*"

Mal picked up the hundred dollar chip, threw it back and if Bello hadn't reached up and caught it in his hand, it would have hit him in the face.

"No tips at this piano."

Bello glowered, and Mal, his hands steady now, and the lump of pain gone from his stomach, began to play the piano intro to the song. Bello's face lost its threatening look; it changed to a smug expression of victory.

The command was obeyed: that was all that mattered to him. He didn't know Mal would play a request for almost anybody—he'd even played this same song for Si Shelby, who'd sat there that night in his open hunting shirt, his money fanned out on the piano in front of him.

Bello stepped back down into the pit, and Mal caught Dee's eye, nodded, gave her the signal: just so she'd be positive he meant it, he motioned with his head, and simultaneously sang:

Come to me, my melancholy baby

Very imperceptibly, she shook her head "no"; and tears she didn't want to show glistened in her eyes. So she was scared, too. She'd thought it over.

Cuddle up and don't be blue.

Bello was back at the table now, and made some remark to her, obviously in reference to Mal, for he pointed at him, then snickered. And Mal pleaded in song, himself surprised at how the lyrics suddenly applied.

All your fears are foolish fancy, maybe

Suddenly she was moving away from the dice table, swiftly, swiftly, as Bello stared after her, his face slowly creasing in great rage: she was coming toward the piano, and Mal kept playing, and now she was almost there, moving very fast, and walked around to the keyboard side, near the portable microphone, and sat on the piano stool with Mal.

There was scarcely a person in the entire room that didn't know the significance of her action, and the buzz of voices was dying: there was a rush of silence. Joe signaled Mal to get Dee off the stool, and started toward them, but Bello snapped:

"No."

It was so quiet now that his voice was heard clearly.

"Dee," he said.

Mal stopped playing.

"Come back here."

There was an even deeper silence. Joe evidently gave the word, and the dice chant and play had stopped at the main table. Out of deference to Bello, so he could make himself heard? As a favor to Mal, who had obviously arranged this? Or was it because of Joe's burning curiosity?

"You heard me, come back here!"

The big man was running a desperate bluff. If she returned, he'd say she was drunk, acting up. But Dee remained on the piano stool.

Joe signaled the pit boss, and the other dice tables quit their play, the chant stopping. Even the clamor of the slot machines and much of the droning babble of the crowd died away. All attention was at the piano. Three hundred people or more were listening, watching. The sudden utter silence was almost unearthly, palling, and Mal thought: the dice have been rolling hour after hour, twenty-four hours a day, ever since the casino opened, so it's historic—this is the day that for a while at least the dice stopped talking. Bello was looking around, uncomfortable, aware of all this, and Joe was watching him with enjoyment and contempt.

Mal picked up the microphone. Dee watched him tensely.

"She's not coming back there any more," Mal said, his voice magnified, "she's staying here with me."

Voice low, Bello snapped at Joe: "Get that man out of the casino."

Through the microphone, Mal said: "I'm leaving. But *she's* coming with me. We're in love, Mr. Bello, and she doesn't want to see you any more. Be the big man the world knows you to be and give us your blessing."

He put the mike down now, placed his arm around Dee, and there was a long, naked silence through the whole casino. Then Bello's voice was heard in what sounded almost like a snarl. He addressed Joe:

"What's the matter with the dice game? Let's get going!"

Joe nodded to the pit boss, and suddenly all of the tables were back in full operation; and a crescendo of voices was heard: the slot machines began to clang again. Everything continued as usual. Up at the piano, Dee was faint.

"Sweetheart, let's get out of here. Let's get out of here right now."

"No, no, if he has the guts to stay doing what he's doing, so do I."

She nodded, but reluctantly; a couple of men edged in close to Bello. And Mal was only half through a song when Joe glanced around and with a nod of his head indicated he should vacate the piano. Only then was Mal scared again. He stopped and climbed to his feet. Dee got up, too, and they left the stand.

Everybody watched them as they walked through the casino and out the door.

They hurried across the lawn toward his bungalow, and Dee was chattering in a kind of terror: "You were right. You see what his pride is? He had to prove to everybody that losing a girl meant nothing to him. He demanded that the dice game go on. That makes him a big man with the public. It meant so little, he just went on playing."

"You sound like *your* pride is hurt."

"Oh, no, I didn't mean it *that* way."

"Joe was a big help. Know that?"

"Yes, wasn't he, though? Does he like you or something?"

"He hates Bello."

"Sweetheart," she said, "you know what we have to do, don't you?"

They were passing the swimming pool. "If you *don't* know," she went on, "this time you'll have to listen to me, and there can be no argument: we have to climb into your car and get out of town as fast as we can."

"Why?"

"Why? Because if you don't, Bello will—"

"He will anyway. If he's going to do anything, he'll find me—no matter where I go."

"But, Mal—"

They stopped, and he looked at her, trying to explain it very gently: "You've done your part—sitting up there with me. My big performance is yet to come. It'll probably be in some dark place and less spectacular, but one goes with the other."

"You mean you're going to stay here and deliberately let him—"

"*You* can go, Diane. I'll send you to Cincinnati and maybe I'll meet you later. I mean, I *will* meet you if—" He was full of fear and couldn't get any more words out. He took her by the hand and led her toward his bungalow. His car was parked on the narrow Rainbow's End street in front.

"I won't go," she said, "I won't leave you. Either we go together or I stay. But, darling, we can both go right now! *Please!*"

"And live in fear? Waiting for the day he—"

The telephone was ringing inside the bungalow. He hurried the remaining steps, unlocked the door and entered. She followed, turning on the lights. He picked up the phone. It was Sprig.

"Hi, Mal," he said, "I don't know what you're doing, but I hope you're planning on leaving these premises in the next few minutes."

"Well, I wasn't, but—"

"Joe doesn't want anything to happen here at Rainbow's End."

"Oh, I see." His voice was flat.

"It'd be bad publicity for us."

"Yeah. I guess it would."

"Since Joe is asking you to leave he says to pay off your full contract; you can pick up your check at the desk on the way out. Okay?"

"Yeah—thank him for me."

"Bello's still at the table. But he's had a couple of side conferences—so I'll be over to watch out for you."

"Thanks, Sprig." He hung up and looked at Dee. "They want me off the property," he said bitterly. "So we'll do it your way. Make a run for it—and let the future take care of itself!"

"Oh, Mal, that's what we *have* to do!"

"So help me pack, will you? They want me to hurry. And what about your stuff?"

"I don't want it. At least half my wardrobe are dresses he bought. Can we afford new clothes for me?"

"Sure we can. We can afford anything for you." He pulled his luggage out of the closet, then set the two pieces on the bed, unlocked them; opened drawers, tore clothes off hangers and in almost no time at all Dee was looking around, saying: "I think that's all, unless—"

"Never mind." He snapped the bags shut, and picked them up. "Let's go."

She opened the door, and he was starting out after her when she suddenly stopped. She was shoved back into the room, and two men came in, one a burly ex-pug and the other wearing a sports jacket over his brown tee shirt. They closed the door.

Mal put the suitcases down very carefully; and Dee screamed.

The men lost no more motion: they converged on Mal. He swung out at them, but the pug smashed him squarely on the jaw and he toppled backward, hitting his head on the end of the bed as he fell. Both men were kicking him in the side and in the stomach. Dee had stopped screaming, and through a blur he saw her rush at the man in the tee shirt. She had taken off one of her shoes, and was pummeling him with the high heel. He swept his arm back, sending her reeling. But she returned, brought the high heel down on the top of his head with a tremendous whack. The tee-shirted man whirled around, hit her viciously with the back of his hand. She fell, bleeding around the mouth, but got up and flew in again to the attack.

Mal didn't see her any more after that because the pug had him pinned to the floor, and was maneuvering to hold him there. Now the man in the tee shirt stooped over and helped. The pug locked Mal's wrist in a grip that was like a vise and with his other hand caught hold of his forefinger, bent it, and then there was a sound like a walnut cracking —and pain rocketed through him; he kept blacking out, and coming to. His middle finger, now his ring finger, then his little finger—the bones in each of them breaking. He struggled wildly, but it was futile. They clutched his other hand. Dee began to scream again: sobbing and screaming both. He couldn't see her very well because everything was a hazy awful red, but she was slashing the shoe at the pug this time. It didn't seem to faze him. He didn't even bother to look up, instead kept religiously to the grim work of cracking walnuts.

Johnny Sprig and Ochoa were leaving the casino when they heard the screams. They broke into a wild sprint, Ochoa drawing his gun. Others were being attracted by the commotion. Bungalow doors were opening, lights going on.

Sprig outran Ochoa, was ten feet ahead of him when

the two men hurried from Mal's room. The one in the tee shirt was holding a gun, ready to blast a way to escape, if necessary. He leveled the weapon at Sprig:

"Stay back!"

Whether it was that Sprig's forward momentum was so great he couldn't stop or that he had so much contempt for these two that the gun didn't scare him, nobody will ever know. Ochoa saw it the most clearly: Sprig kept running—straight at the gun. There was a shot and Sprig fell forward, still running. Ochoa opened fire, his bullet going through tee shirt's face. The pug threw up his hands. A crowd was hurrying over from the casino.

Ochoa knelt by Sprig, pulled him over on his back, and then began to cry, hot tears searing his cheeks. "Boss... *boss!*"

Sprig was dead.

Thirty-four

He lay face up in the grass, his eyes still open, and kneeling there over him, Joe tried to say goodbye, but couldn't even *think* it silently, because he could not believe Sprig was really dead; Johnny Sprig, the indestructible! Finally he stood up, numbly, his whole body numb, his mind numb, and was looking at Ochoa. The Mexican was wet-eyed, full of rage and grief and burning with a great bitterness. When he spoke it was in a half whisper.

"He was right about Miss Guido."

Joe didn't hear at first, and Ochoa repeated it: "He was right about the girl. I just got back from San Francisco a few minutes ago. She was planted on you, just as he suspected."

Rage was billowing into Joe. "What are you talking about?"

Ochoa was staring down at Sprig. "He was always right about things."

Joe grabbed him. *"What are you talking about?"*

Casino police were keeping the crowd several feet back. A sheriff's car, its siren whining, moved into the street.

Ochoa looked up, then gazed out at the crowd. "Why don't you ask *her,* Mr. Martin?"

Joe was still too dazed to comprehend. It was too incredible: too much was happening all at the same time. "Ask her *what?*"

"The things Mr. Sprig wanted to ask her."

Now it was coming through to him. "Are you trying to tell me—"

"I talked to her father today. He thinks you killed one of his sons. She probably does, too."

"Sunny—*Sunny Guido* was—"

Ochoa nodded.

Joe's face contorted. He was so livid that for a moment he could not speak again, could not move. Then suddenly he was brushing past Ochoa, going into the crowd, searching for Sunny. When he found her he walked straight over and gripped her by the shoulders. But he still couldn't talk and people were staring at them. Joe caught her by the arm, started walking her toward the parking lot.

When they were alone, he backed her up against a car. "Now tell me."

"Joe, I can explain—"

Those words shattered his last hope that it wasn't true. "Just tell me! Tell me whether it's true. Was Sprig right? *Were* you a plant? Sent here to—"

Tears streaming, she nodded.

It took him several more moments to absorb it.

"But I can—"

"Don't talk, Sunny!"

She shrank from the look she saw on his face. "What are you—"

"I'm going to kill you."

"Joe—"

"I told you—*don't talk!*"

She kept crying. "If you'd listen—"

"There's nothing to listen to! Oh, you roped me in, all right. Roped me in good! Real professional job! The virgin schoolteacher from—"

"THAT'S ALL TRUE!"

"Sure. Everything's true. Everything's true. You slut! You miserable conniving doll-faced slut! Took me for a two million dollar sleigh ride. I'm up humping a Wop while Bello's gouging out my life's blood. Sure, everything's true. Johnny Sprig is dead. That's true, too."

"If you're going to kill me—do it!"

"Shut up! Shut up your whore's mouth!"

"I said do it!"

He grabbed her violently, ripped at her dress. "No, I'll make it ten thousand times *worse*. Trust me—I'll make it worse than a quick, cheap, easy way out. Right now get your ass up to the penthouse and stay there. And don't try to leave—the security police'll have orders to stop you." He gave her a shove. "Go on now, get going."

Sobbing, she started for the casino.

Doc Hoffman had just finished bandaging Mal's hands. They were in his bungalow office. He'd treated Dee, too, for minor injury, and then she'd gone to Bello's bungalow. The suite was deserted, so she'd changed from her torn dress into slacks; and since there was no longer the great need to hurry, packed a bag with her own clothes after all—a white wool coat, cotton skirts and blouses—inexpensive things she had owned before she met Bello. The suitcase was standing on the sidewalk beside the white Cad convertible now and she was in here with Mal and Doc.

Mal felt better. The abrasions on his face were not serious—didn't even need adhesive; he had two cracked ribs on the right side, but they were taped up so tightly he felt as if he were wearing a corset; and the eight broken fingers, four on each hand, were in splints.

"You won't be playing piano for a while."

"How long, Doc? I've saved asking you that because— I guess I'm afraid of the answer."

"If they knit well, and there's no reason why they shouldn't, you'll be able to use your fingers again in six or seven months."

"I can play then?"

"Probably not as well as usual. But give them a year and you'll be right back in your old form. They're all clean breaks. Now if the fingers had been mashed, it'd be a different story. You're lucky to be alive."

"I'll say I'm lucky."

Doc smiled at Dee. "Wish I'd been in the casino when he gave his version of Washington's farewell to his troops."

She nodded thoughtfully. "The dice chant stopped for almost a full minute."

"Yes, that was a big thing."

"And Sprig's dead because of it," Mal said bitterly.

"Don't think of it that way. He died doing his job. It could have happened a hundred different ways."

Mal looked at Dee now, holding up his splinted fingers.

"Isn't really bad as it seems. One of the big record companies wants me to make an album using voice only. I'll do it now. And maybe I can even get some night club bookings with that bit. Sitting on a high stool, back-stopped with music, and just singing."

Doc Hoffman smiled warmly. "The undespairing soul of man. Break the fingers he uses to earn his bread and he finds another way home."

He walked them out to the car, put Dee's white leather suitcase into the back seat. She slid behind the wheel and Mal lingered on the sidewalk a moment.

"Doc, it's been a pleasure knowing you." Then he suddenly remembered: "I haven't paid you for fixing me up."

"It's on the house. Comes out of my resident-physician's fee. It's been a pleasure knowing you, too, Malcolm."

A few minutes later, the white convertible was on the highway, driving along the Strip, passing the giant, sparkling signs of the Flamingo, The Sands, Sahara, Tropicana, Thunderbird, Riviera, Royal Nevada, Desert Inn, Stardust, El Rancho Vegas, and all the flamboyant neon monuments to the lavish motels that vied for space in this gaudy kaleidoscopic skyline.

"Here's one town I'll never see again," Dee said softly. "Where to, Mal?"

"East. New York City—where else? And Diane, on the way, let's stop off and be married in every state we pass through, except this one. Even if some have a three-day waiting period. We're in no big hurry—we'll just sit there and wait."

The Cad moved a little faster now, and he didn't look at the signs any more.

She laughed. "You want to *really* nail me down, don't you?"

"You know it."

"Goes vice versa," she said.

Thirty-five

5:03 A.M.

When Joe at last returned to the gambling pit, an excited murmur passed through the room, and then, except for the dice chant, it was almost quiet. He took his place on the other side of the table from Bello, his eyes boring into the older man.

"I warned you not to pull anything in my casino."

"I didn't," Bello said coldly.

"YOU'RE A LIAR!"

Bello stiffened. "If you want to use that accusation as an excuse to quit this game—"

"Who's quitting?"

Bello stared at him. Joe motioned the pit boss over. "This table is closed to everybody except Mr. Bello."

"All right," the pit boss said, "you heard him, folks. This table is shut down."

The customers picked up their chips, moved back a little, impressed; no one complained. Bello was watching, wondering.

"We don't need the crew," Joe said.

The stickman, money man and others walked away as spectators now thronged around, six deep. In the background, a few people were even standing on the rungs of bar stools.

"We buck heads, that it?" Bello asked.

"Yeah, just the two of us. A back alley crap game." There was fury in Joe's voice and he made sure he could be heard by the onlookers. "I'll fade you for any amount of money you want to name. The only stipulation is, you do the same for me."

Bello hesitated.

"You're not backing down, Mr. Bello?"

"No."

"Good thing, Mr. Bello. If you ever back down from any gambling game, you're through. You're pretty much aware of that, aren't you, Mr. Bello?"

Bello picked up a pair of dice. "Let's get started."

"No, *I'll* shoot first," Joe said. "You've been throwing those dice for three days and nights. Now it's my turn."

"We'll roll high die for it."

Joe threw out a single die. Five. Bello rolled out a die. Six.

"All right, you roll first," Joe conceded.

Bello held two dice in his hand and called for the last tally.

"Million seven hundred thousand four hundred fifty— *your* plus," the pit boss told him.

"I'm coming out for fifty thousand dollars."

There was a gasp from the spectators as the chips were placed.

"You're faded."

Bello rolled a five, and then rolled several times more, trying to make another five, but Joe didn't even watch; his temples were throbbing, his mouth felt dry; all he could think was Sunny, Sunny, Sunny, Sunny! And he was falling apart inside. He felt so much pain, such absolute despair that he wanted to yell out at the top of his voice.

"There it is," Bello said.

Joe looked down and saw a three and a two. "Your point. Now you're a million and three-quarters in. How much are you coming out for?"

"Hundred thousand."

"Bet."

Bello rolled a seven.

"Million, eight hundred and fifty thousand and odd cents," Joe said.

Bello said: "A hundred and fifty G's minus the odd dollars. If I make it, we'll be at two million even."

"You're faded."

Joe watched as Bello shook the big dice in his sweaty hand, then threw them hard against the far backboard. He saw the six and five.

"Eleven, winner," Joe said, imitating a stickman. "Now what do you shoot?"

"You really want to go on this way?"

"Yeah—I really do."

"Back to fifty."

"Go."

Bello rolled a six, got it right back.

"Two million, fifty thousand," said Joe, his face set. The spectators were almost afraid to breathe.

"Fifty once more," said Bello.

"Piker."

"Isn't enough for you?"

"Not nearly."

"I'm happy," Bello said.

He rolled an eight.

"Eight, easy eight," he purred, rolling a four.

"No side bets?" Joe asked.

"No; we're bucking heads." Bello threw the dice. "Five and three," he said.

They came up four and three.

He looked at Joe: "We're back to two million even. Your dice."

Joe picked up the same dice Bello had used and looked straight at him.

"I'm coming out for one million dollars."

There was an uproar in the pit.

Bello looked as if someone had hit him in the face. "Wait a minute—"

"You agreed to fade any bet I made."

"I didn't agree to gamble with a madman."

The babble of voices died and silence hung in the air; the excitement in the crowd was at a terrible surging pitch. All eyes were on the table.

"Am I faded or not?"

Bello gazed around the room, then back at Joe. Sweat was coming on his neck. "Look—"

"Faded or not?"

"Shoot!"

Joe rolled an eleven.

Three days, three nights, endless hours making complicated bets, going without sleep, sometimes without food—and in one throw of the dice he had wiped out a million dollars' worth of that suffering!

"Coming out again," Joe said, "same bet. One million dollars."

Bello started to open his mouth, but no words came out. The big red dice hit the table, bounced against the backboard. *Four.* One of the two hardest numbers to make.

Bello was able to breathe again.

Joe rolled a five, then a six, then an eight, then eight again. On the next roll, the dice flipped off the backboard, landed on the green felt table and lay there, motionless, showing a pair of twos.

Joe looked into Bello's unbelieving eyes. "We're even now. But once *more* for one million dollars."

Bello shook his head violently. "No, I'm through!"

"If you're out of money, I'll take a note."

"No," Bello said harshly, "I've had enough!"

"*I* haven't," Joe said flatly.

"What do you mean?"

"You weren't playing for yourself."

"Did I ever say I was?"

"How much did they bankroll you?"

"Four hundred thousand."

"Cashier's check—local bank?"

Bello nodded.

Joe said: "Put it on the table."

Bello reached for his wallet. "You want to roll for it?"

"No. The boys who backed you are buying a very expensive tombstone for a man named Sprig."

Bello hesitated, then read death in Joe's eyes; and saw the faces of security men in the crowd. It wasn't his money anyway. He put the check for four hundred thousand dollars on the green felt of the dice table. He started to go, but someone blocked his way.

"One thing more," Joe said.

Bello looked up.

"What syndicate? What city?"

"They didn't tell me."

Joe stared straight into his eyes.

"My contact was a Mr. Wily."

"Now dead."

"Is he?" said Bello, "I didn't know. I've been busy playing craps. But *he's* the only one who could have told you. Now I guess nobody'll ever know what syndicate it was, in what city—or the names of any of the men running it. But there's something to remember, Mr. Martin—it can start again tomorrow, or next week, or next month, or next year—whenever they or some other group feel up to it. Maybe they'll be smarter next time, or stronger—and maybe you'll be weaker. Without Mr. Sprig you're bound to be weaker. He was your strength. He was the backbone of Rainbow's End. My play is over for now—but yours'll never end."

Bello turned and walked away.

Joe stood absolutely motionless for a moment, then looked over at his pit boss.

"Open this table up again."

He headed for the penthouse.

When he opened the door, Sunny was there. She had changed to a traveling suit and was trying to close down the lid of a hastily crammed suitcase. He shut the door, moved toward her.

"I told you—you're not going anywhere!"

She faced him. "Joe, will you *listen?* Now will you listen?"

He moved away from her. "The big game is over."

"A Mr. Wily came to our house in San Francisco…"

"I beat him."

"He told my family that my brother Al—that you murdered my brother Al three years ago…"

"Beat *him*—and *all* of them—the unknowns—with their tricks and stunts."

"He said all I had to do was be nice to you." His back was to her, and she moved up to it. "I didn't have to report to anybody, to spy—anything like that. Just be nice to you. And the thing is, when I realized it had all been a trick—"

He swung around, facing her. "I *hit* Sprig because of you!" Now he moved past her again. "God, I'm tired! I've never been this tired." He stretched out in a leather lounge chair, lit a cigarette and gazed at the orange flame of the match in his shaky hand. "So you got conned, is that it? You got conned by Wily. Well, you wouldn't be hard to con. *I* conned you, didn't I? I conned you all the way."

She knelt on the floor and took his hand, and looked up, ready to speak.

"No," he said, "no more. Tomorrow maybe. I'm too

tired. I'm sure it's a sad story and that you were innocent. You're too dumb to be anything else. But I just don't want to talk about it now." He sucked hard for his breath.

She whispered: "I love you."

"Well, you're in for it then. If this is going to be your life. Because I don't want that boat I talked about—or any trips. Not until I get old. I want Rainbow's End. And if you're going to be Mrs. Rainbow's End, you're in for it. Because the big siege can start again any time. Tomorrow, next week, next month—any time."

The cigarette dropped from his fingers. She picked it up from the rug and carefully put it out.

Steve Fisher's *No House Limit*

AN AFTERWORD BY ONE OF HIS SONS

If you were looking for glamour and excitement, gambling, sex and entertainment, then Las Vegas in the mid-1950's was the place to be. It was an almost magical oasis of hotels and casinos out in the middle of the desert. The Flamingo, Thunderbird, El Rancho Vegas, Tropicana, Sands, Riviera and Sahara. The most amazing part was that less than seven years earlier none of these world-class resorts had even existed. Up until then Las Vegas had just been a dusty little town on the way to Los Angeles. Then one day a murderous, if imaginative, gangster named Bugsy Siegel had an idea and changed all that. And the rest was history. (But as remarkable and eventually as successful as Mr. Siegel's vision had been... success for the Flamingo Hotel and Casino didn't come in time to save his life. On June 20, 1946, his unhappy partners had him killed at his home in Beverly Hills, just three blocks down from where our family was living at the time.)

By the early 1950s Las Vegas was drawing visitors from all over the world and especially from Los Angeles and Hollywood. Movie stars were to be seen everywhere. Top entertainers were making $30,000 a week. Beautiful showgirls and starlets hoped to be discovered. High rollers won and lost fortunes on a nightly basis. My father, who wrote this book, knew many of these people as they chased their hopes and dreams and coped with their desperations.

My dad loved the excitement of Las Vegas…and for that matter just liked to gamble, whether it was horse racing, gin rummy at a nickel a point, or ping pong on the back patio…or as he and some other writers working at the studios liked to do, pitching silver dollars to fill out a morning until lunch. And I can remember hot Sunday afternoons and evenings at our house in the San Fernando Valley when he would spread a "Green Crap Table Cloth" with all the markings on the floor. Then he would be the Bank for a crap game with myself and my brother and sister and maybe a dozen or more neighborhood kids (we had the only swimming pool in the area, which made us more or less headquarters)…and if we lost our nickels and dimes and quarters and later asked him for more money, he would sigh in mock exasperation and offer us such sage advice as, "You have to stop squandering your money on things like food and rent."

So the attraction to write a novel about Las Vegas was no surprise…and writing is what he did best. By then he had published somewhere between 90 and 100 novels and over 900 short stories and had written 120 or so movies and episodes of television series. In later years other writers would tell me that, because of his output, they used to think Steve Fisher was a corporation and that there had to be at least four or five people writing under that name.

He had no way of knowing, of course, how unique a time it was in Las Vegas. Looking back, one can see it was almost a generational period. The small, dusty town Las Vegas had been was long gone. Bugsy Siegel's vision and eventual brutal murder and the hard feelings it generated were finally settling. It was a time when the other (Syndicate-run) hotels were ready to flex their muscles and think about expansion...which meant going after the real-world equivalents of Joe Martin's "Rainbow's End Hotel and Casino," the biggest, the best and most glamorous hotel casinos on the strip.

Again, one can catch a glimpse of the generational change-over. Las Vegas in the early 1950's was headed for the (yet unseen) future of mega-corporations, resorts and casinos run within a corporate structure. But Joe was in effect a lone wolf. He was like a Bogart character in a movie. He stood alone against the enemy, running the Rainbow's End in Las Vegas much like Bogart ran Rick's Place in *Casablanca*.

My father wrote two films for Humphrey Bogart, *Dead Reckoning* and *Tokyo Joe*. As I recall, they were pretty good friends in the period they worked together...and if you look, there are several times in the book when Joe Martin's dialogue sounds very much like a Bogart line out of a movie...page 35, for instance, when he's in an argument with Sunny, the girl he he's attracted to but doesn't trust:

> *"Joe, I didn't mean it the way it sounded."*
> *"Mean what?"* he demands.
> *"I didn't mean to hurt you."*
> *"Nobody hurts me,"* he replies.

I know we've all seen a lot of Bogart films, but an exchange like that, scalding words in a tense scene between a cynical man and a beautiful woman...just feels very Bogart to me. There are at least a half a dozen other spots scattered throughout.

As noted before, my father was a very prolific writer. He was also very disciplined. Whether it was a novel or a

movie he would block the story out scene by scene on
3-by-5 cards, which he would pin on the walls around his
desk. When they were complete (which might take weeks
—but rarely did) he'd pound out at least a chapter a day
until done.

On *No House Limit* his notes would read something
like…

> *Chapter 1: The book centers around Joe Martin and
> the "Rainbow's End Hotel and Casino," which he
> owns. The biggest, gaudiest and best casino hotel
> on the strip. As the story opens, Joe is aware that
> "trouble" is coming. He's not sure what it is or where
> it's coming from, he just knows that the last few days,
> people have been watching him.*

> *Chapter 2: Meet Sunny. Unlike the showgirls and
> hookers…Sunny is a schoolteacher from Utah…her
> good looks and innocence attract Joe. "I would trade
> the casino for her," he was heard to muse.*

> *Chapter 3: Meet some of the interesting people in the
> casino including Mal who plays the piano and sings in
> the lounge.*

(Like most writers, my father would at times use real
people as the basis for a character. Mal was based on
Matt Dennis, a famous lounge singer and composer. He
wrote songs such as "Angel Eyes," "Violets for Your Furs,"
and some early Frank Sinatra hits, among many others.
He played for years and years in various clubs in Los
Angeles. Matt Dennis was a friend of my father's.)

> *Chapter 4: Report…Counterfeit chips are flooding
> into the casino. Joe knows that the assault on his empire
> had begun.*

$500 million over his lifetime, going from rags to
s and back again over seventy times.

some ways Nick the Greek and his giant wins and
exemplifies a great deal of what Las Vegas is…but
o do the showgirls and the entertainers. The gam-
winning or losing, taking their big chance. It's a
l place of dreams. Hope and desperation.

House Limit captures a great deal of this, and I
y father would be pleased to see it back in print.

— Michael Fisher

Chapter 6: BELLO arrives. Bello is a [...]
bler. But even he wouldn't come after J[...]
Joe quickly understands that Bello is [...]
"someone…or some group of peop[...]
take over the Rainbow's End. Bell[...]
"hired gun."

Like the character of Mal, the cha[...]
roots in a real-life person…in this[...]
gambler named Nicholas Dand[...]
as "Nick the Greek." Dandolos[...]
character who dressed all in bla[...]
novel). In 1951 the real Nick th[...]
one poker non-stop for four mo[...]
is told he lost a million and a [...]
believe that game was the insp[...]
of Poker.

I remember meeting Nic[...]
was researching this book. [...]
home, then in the San F[...]
where we ended up, but[...]
patch of dusty, desolate[...]
was in Las Vegas.) Once[...]
out to the barn where t[...]
ters. If the glamour o[...]
hadn't already started[...]
were for the most pa[...]
who needed money[...]
to save their home[...]
five or ten dollars [...]
gamble with it ur[...]
desperate need. V[...]
was that on any g[...]
one of his "brok[...]

leas[...]
rich[...]
In [...]
losses[...]
then s[...]
blers [...]
magica[...]
No [...]
know m[...]